What people are saying about Mikasenoja's debut novel
"The First Lady: Confessions of a Preacher's Wife"

The First Lady: Confessions of a Preacher's Wife is a great reality check and learning tool for current and future Preacher's Wives. It shows the discerning growth and trust in God needed for this crucial and special spot for God's first ladies to uphold God's leading man."
Camellia Johnson, Dallas, TX, author of "What Now?"

"Finally...a heart-felt, passionate treatment by a real pastor's wife for the real pastor's wife. Like Queen Esther, Mikasenoja has been anointed to deliver such a word of brilliance and breakthrough to the most neglected and often most wounded area of the church... the pastor's wife. Read with determination, read with discernment, read for divine deliverance!"
Pastor Mike Stevens, University City Church, Charlotte, North Carolina, <u>www.theuniversitychurch.com</u>

Thank you, Mikasenoja, for your insight and honesty when reflecting on the life of the preacher's wife. This work is true to life and a reminder of our humble calling, a servant. Thank you for reminding us to be prayful and steadfast for the sake of God's Kingdom.
Regina Randall, First Lady of Greater St. Matthew BC Hitchcock, TX

"As a ministers' wife, this book has proven to be riveting and exfoliating yet enlightening, cleansing, rejuvenating and restoring. Not unless you have walked down Clergy Wife Avenue, will you be able to feel her world. "The First Lady: Confessions of a Preacher's Wife" allows the reader to not only feel these unique women, but to actually experience their world. My prayer is that this book will turn hearts to become bonafide prayer coverers for these Women of God."
Darlene Ephriam – Temple Restoration Consulting, Austin, Texas <u>www.templerest.org</u>

"Finally, a textbook for minister's wives! 'The First Lady' should be on the bookshelf of every pastor's wife in the country. The real life problems and situations will have everyone examining themselves to see if they resemble any of the characters in the book. This straight from the hip work details the hardships, doubts and pitfalls that are the proving ground for faith, courage and spiritual maturity required of pastor's wives to survive on the front lines of the battlefield that we call the Church."

> *Jeanette W. Hill, Playwright Sight Ain't Seeing Productions*
> *THE BROOM, IT'S NOT ABOUT YOU*

"Great fiction! Good book!"

> *Mary Varner, First Lady of Bible Way Baptist Fellowship*
> *Church, Houston, TX*

"This book challenges the minister's wife to become a consistent prayer warrior and sincerely, spiritually see the pitfalls that hinder us. The heroine, Mrs. Jacqueline Stevens, is a phenomenal, awesome woman of God, because she knows where her strength comes from. Her help comes from the Lord! Every woman in the church can learn something from Sister Stevens."

> *Cindy Wright, minister's wife of Community Baptist Church,*
> *Texas City, TX*

"This work is awesome! It is true to life!"

> *Rosalie Wicks, former First Lady of Olivet Baptist Church*
> *for 30 years, Austin, TX*

The First Lady: Confessions of a Preacher's Wife

BY MIKASENOJA

1663 LIBERTY DRIVE, SUITE 200
BLOOMINGTON, INDIANA 47403
(800) 839-8640
WWW.AUTHORHOUSE.COM

First published by AuthorHouse 09/09/05

ISBN: 1-4208-8429-8 (sc)

Library of Congress Control Number: 2005908183

Printed in the United States of America
Bloomington, Indiana

This book is printed on acid-free paper.

Artwork on front cover by Art Teacher, Desiree Haddock

Dedicated to my parents,
Minister Fred Jones I 1949-1997
&
Lois Henderson Jones
You gave me the love of life and laughter and taught
me to always make the best of any situation.
Even in this…always give praise to God!

Table of Contents

Acknowledgements

"For with God nothing shall be impossible," Luke 1:37. This scripture has propelled me to discover my full potential in Christ Jesus who without Him this literary work would not be possible. I give Jesus all of the praise and adoration for choosing me to deliver a message of hope, love and restoration. I want to thank my husband, Pastor C.L. Yancy, Sr. for all of your unconditional love and unwavering support toward my literary career and other ministry opportunities. You are the wind beneath my wings! I adore your honesty and your desire to help me reach my destiny in Christ. To my children, Joshua, William Caleb, Jennifer and Clinton Jr.; my precious treasures -thank you for allowing mommy to share her gift with the world and for your patience with me while I was "away" writing. Remember, only what you do for Christ will last. To my parents, the late Minister Fred Jones and my mother Lois Jones, I thank you both for instilling in me a gift of service and love toward Kingdom Building. I love you, Mama for instilling in me the importance of a consistent, persistent prayer life. This book is for you! You are the epitome of a WOW woman; a Woman of the Word, a Woman of Wisdom and a Woman of Worship. I love you! To my only sibling and younger brother, Minister Fred Jones II and family, thank you for always believing in your older sister and giving me countless words of wisdom. You are a phenomenal man in Christ! I am waiting on your book to come out! To the Henderson, Jones, Stevens, Mays, Mercer, Prosser, Clark, Yancy, Greenhouse, Haddock families thank you for the strong rich Christian heritage that I have gained from all of you. To my favorite aunt, who never stops believing in me, El-nita Simmons & family – you are my strength and I love you! To my mother-in-law, a pastor's wife who challenged me to stand strong, thank you! You taught me how to be tough. You were the first to in-troduce me to the world of Christian fiction! To my armor bearer, Sister Gussie Dawsey, thank you for covering me in prayer through the years and encouraging me to stay true to my purpose. You are a cheerleader for the Christian faith! To Ron DeShay, Arvis Watts, Dedrick Johnson, and Kiki Jones for helping me to discover the gift of purpose within me and pushing me out here to tell the story and to give God Glory. To my late godmother, Mildred Vorsburgh; thank you for always making me feel special, anointed and appointed for a time such as this. To Sharon Johnson, my faithful prayer warrior, you seemed to fill the void after the passing of my precious god-mother. You all are my inspiration! To Desiree Haddock, your book cover design is awesome! You are the best kept secret in Galveston County! To my sorors of Delta Sigma Theta Sorority, Inc. thank you so much for your continued support of my efforts. To all of my Uni-versity of Texas at Austin alumni, students, faculty, and staff thank you for your standard of excellence in all things.

To my literary friends across the nation who counseled me, prayed for me and encouraged me. Thank you so much! To my team of edi-tors, Wanda Lartique, Arvis Watts, Tamara Glaspie, and Canditha Davis, you are the best editing team the world has seen!! Thanks to Marilyn Long of Vision Ink LLC who invested so much of her time and wisdom toward this project. God directed you into my life just in the nick of time! Thanks to the Pageturner.Net network and Pamela Williams for your excellent web and networking services. Thank you, Bishop Terry and the Gospel Magazine family for the opportunity to write for the Lord. To my gospel music friends and gospel announcers across the nation who I have had the pleasure of sharing my life with, thank you so much for your music inspiration which is the back drop of this project. To all of my high school English teachers and college professors thank you for recognizing a gift of prose in me and challenging me to reach new heights in writing. To my colleagues and students of LaMarque ISD thank you so much for your unfailing support and encouragement toward this labor of love.

To the church families that I have been blessed to share affiliation with from Munger Avenue, Mt. Carmel, Mt. Sinai, and New Hope, thank you for the medium of the church where I have found peace, deliverance, joy and sometimes pain but ultimately I found the truth; that there is a reality in serving a true and living God. To all of my church families, senior pastors, and wise first ladies, I sincerely love you!

Thanks to all of the people who have sown a seed into my life, whether financially or wise counsel. Your seeds have been vested into good ground! May God receive the glory! Thank you to all of the pastors, ministers, clergy wives, mission sisters and brothers who covered this book with prayer.

Thanks in advance to all of the persons, book clubs, book store owners, and librarians, who will read this literary work and pass on the good news!

And finally to all of the ministers' wives and clergy who shared their testimonies, endorsement and their labor of love, thank you for your encouragement. To my sisters in the Grand Ole East Association, thank you for your blessings and prayers. To the attendees of Yancy Ministries Powershop Clergy Wives conferences thank you for your support toward the purpose of this ministry literary work.

And again I want to thank God for the power of the pen to restore and heal. I want to thank him for the cross and salvation! Praise be to God!

Because of Calvary, we remain
        Kimberley Nicole Yancy
        aka - Mikasenoja

Foreword

"What Is Our Crime?"

The Senior Pastor's wife has been accused of being too bold, because she has a healthy self esteem. And, she has been accused of being too stand-offish, because she suffers from an un-healthy self esteem. But the truth of the matter is she will never receive an honest chance, because she's the pastor's wife.

It is a sad and tragic fact that so many innocent women are targeted and made miserable because she is married to the pastor. Is this supposed to be her crime? If so, why? Should a pastor's wife be mistreated because she married a preacher? If this is the case, then we should expect pastors' wives to mistreat members because of their choices? Yet, it seems that some members believe they are exempt from heeding what the word says. But God's word states "they that plow iniquity, and sow wickedness, reap the same" (Job 4:8). Then, it says in Galatians 6:7, "Be not deceived; God is not mocked: for whatsoever a man soweth, that shall he also reap." If these members were not under such an impression then they would not spend countless hours striving to make the pastor's wife's life miserable.

But the saddest thing of all, these women are under the impression that they're going to be the replacement. What they fail to realize is the pastor's wife has grown through years of dealing with such games. Therefore, she has gained a lot of experience and wisdom from the games that have been played. The games are so easy to spot and the players are recognizable, too. It is amazing that it doesn't change from one church to another. The game is the same, even though the players may change. Satan has not put into play a new or different game that pastors' wives haven't already been exposed to.

The majority of pastors' wives have learned more about political strategies in the churches where their husbands have served than anywhere else. They have been exposed to the oldest, the latest, and the most cleaver games played. Yet, God has kept them sane, even though, they have seen and heard it all; from the bringing in of women to entice the pastor, to the using of associate minister's wives to spite, and hurt her. It is a well known fact that the pastor's wife is made a target as soon as she arrives. And, it does not matter how sweet or pleasant she may be.

It is truly sad that so many pastors' wives have had to suffer at the hands of church folks for so long. Some have chosen to leave their husbands rather than put up with such nonsense. Others have suffered ill health and mental anguish. But there are some who have decided to uncover and expose the bad treatment of pastor's wives, and our hats are off to them. Yet, the ultimate question that pastors' wives are asking all over this country, "What is our crime?"

The heroine of this novel, Jacqueline Stevens, reminds us that there is hope for the Pastor's Wife if we stay with God and stay the course.

Written by First Lady Fannie P. Mays, a Senior Pastor's wife for over 35 years.
From the Heart

Chapter 1

A Fresh New Start

I walked into the church and peeked at the pale green pews, the nostalgic pipe organ, the fresh green carpet, the newly polished pulpit and prayed that this experience would be different. You see, my husband was just appointed pastor of the New Light Church in Southlake, Texas, right outside the Dallas/Fort Worth, area. This was our first official visit as pastor and pastor's wife. My husband has been pastoring for over 12 years now and we have both had our ups and downs. Funny, I never thought it would have been this way. I never envisioned my life in a fishbowl; a life under constant scrutiny, where people are looking in and I am captured in a bowl of unspoken boundaries. Church was a place of safety and refuge and a place away from the world's darts and fears. However, many times I have run away from the church. I have run away from its accusations, its definitions, and its people. After all, the church is defined as, "a body of believers." Well, those so called bible packing believers have run many people away from the church house.

"Well, Mrs. Stevens, we have heard so much about you and all of your many talents. We are so excited to have you as our first lady," said a middle-aged woman with a tight pink hat on, with matching pink gloves and a pink suit. "My name is Sarah Finley and my husband is Deacon Abraham Finley; we are one of the founding families of the New Light Church. I was six years old or maybe two years old, you know I rarely discuss my age, when New Light was founded by my great grandfather, Pastor S. L. Robinson. Yes, I remember those struggles to keep these church doors open, and all those chickens that were slaughtered for dinner plates. I think New Light sold every part of the chicken to bring some money in the Lord's house," said Sister Finley with a look of nostalgia and sweet memories as she thought about New Light's historic past.

"Is there anything that you need at this time? How do you like your parsonage? The deacon's wives and I took the time, last month, to decorate it, just to let you know how much we are looking forward to having you, Pastor Stevens and your children. Was everything the way you like it, Mrs. Stevens, or would you like me to call you, First Lady?"

"Oh, Mrs. Finley the house is beautiful and Sister Stevens would be just fine," I nodded to her in respect. I smoothed out my conservative size 12 peach linen A-line dress which hung slightly below my knees, with matching 2 ½ inch peach Fioni high heeled sandals which I wore to meet with Sister Finley. I wore my shoulder length dyed jet blue-black hair in a slicked back bun to appear more conservative as this was only my second time meeting with Sister Finley. I wanted to make sure to leave a good impression, so I wore my Tiffany inspired faux peach Indian jewelry with matching earrings, necklace, and bracelet. I topped the look off with a peach clutch Fendi bag, which I held stiffly by my side. The peach dress and matching accessories gave my brown chestnut skin a gorgeous glow.

"I must say, First Lady, you are looking quite dainty today. I like your sense of style. It is just what our New Light needs, a pastor's wife with some class," said Sister Finley.

"Thank you so much, Sister Finley. And please, please, you can call me Sister Stevens," I responded.

Though I was most honored by being called First Lady, I knew and understood that it is just a term of endearment and in many ways it is paradoxical anyway. Typically the term "First Lady" is used for formal occasions, and besides, the way Sister Finley had just said First Lady, it sounded more like a sarcastic question.

"Please tell the Deacons' Wives Ministry how grateful I am for their assistance." The church ladies had decorated the parsonage in a soft baby blue and pastel green. Last night, my husband and I almost had a "slight discussion" because the first thing I wanted him to do was to call a contractor to paint the parsonage a color that I could live with. Baby blue and pastel green, yuk! Lord, please give me patience and Lord, forgive me for lying in this church house that everything was beautiful with our parsonage. I have learned that sometimes it is just better to be grateful for what you have. Hence, the politically correct response with a Star Jones smile, "Everything was beautiful, thanks so much."

I pray for a time when we can purchase our own house, choose our own colors and have our own furniture. The first parsonage we lived in had a roof full of leaks and during the first three months every time it rained, which was at least once a week, we had to put pots all over the house. It took the deacons forever to get a contractor to come out and fix the leaks in the roof. And Lord, bless my husband, but he is truly just a preacher and not a maintenance man.

My husband's name is Lance McClain Stevens, I. He has been preaching the gospel since he was 23 years old. He is a third generation preacher. His father and grandfather were both preachers. He has pastored two churches and now he is beginning his third pastorate. We have three children, Connie, Jaylyn and Lance Jr., ages 7, 10 and 13. Lance and I have been married for 16 years. We met at the University of Texas at Austin. He was director of the gospel choir and I sang a mean first soprano. After several dates, we fell madly in love and we have been together ever since.

I never dreamt of being a pastor's wife or minister's wife. I just dreamed of falling in love with a man who loved Christ as much as I did. At first when Lance asked me for a date, I declined, because everybody knew that Lance would be a preacher/pastor one day and I didn't want that life. Too many times, I had seen pastors' wives give up their dreams and careers and somehow lose themselves for the sake of the ministry and their husband's ambitious ministry goals. Besides, I felt that pastors' wives were either too skinny or too fat and point blank I didn't want to be one of them.

Yes, I know I had a stereotypical view of pastors' wives, but I never wanted to be in their sorority. So I ran away from Lance's offers of courtship for over a year and a half. He was very persistent, so I finally went on a date with him. I found him to be very easy to talk to about God and that we had so much in common. After the first date I was somewhat hooked on his character and integrity. So I agreed to see him, again and again. Now here we are over 19 years later, now married with three children and a church to lead.

"Sister Stevens, Sister Stevens," said Sister Finley.

"Oh, I am sorry, Sister Finley, I guess I just dazed off. What were you saying?"

"We are sponsoring a 'Meet the First Lady' tea next month and we want to know what your favorite colors are?"

"Well, I am partial to royal purple or lavender and millennium silver."
"Don't you think that purple is too strong of a color, my dear?"
"Pastel lavender will do just fine, Sister Finley."

"My thoughts exactly First Lady, oops, Sister Stevens. Well, I must be going. My Cadillac has to be serviced today and I can't be late, but if there is anything else you need, here is my card with my home number, cell phone, and pager. Welcome, First Lady, to our beloved New Light."

"Thank you, Sister Finley." I watched her as she strutted down the aisle of the church as if she had done her duty and now was off to the next matter at hand.

As she walked out of the sanctuary, I saw my husband walk in with his eye looking up into the high vaulted ceilings of New Light.
"How do you like the church, honey? Isn't it beautiful?" said Lance walking down the center aisle of the sanctuary with his arms outstretched.

I looked at my 40-year-old, 6'3, 215 lbs, ebony King and quietly exhaled. After all these years, this mahogany creature could still light my fire. Lance looked like he was born to lead this church. This morning, he was wearing a linen Sean John brown casual outfit with a white tank underneath and brown sandals that displayed his size

12 shoe size. Lance could have easily browsed the covers of Ebony and GQ, with his tall stature and gorgeous pearly white teeth that he meticulously brushed at least twice a day. He still jogged at least four miles a week to maintain his physical contour. I draped my arms around his neck, and kissed him lightly on the lips.

"Yes, sweetheart, New Light is beautiful. I love the wooden interiors of the church. It makes it look so classic," I said.

We looked at the interior of the church sanctuary, which could easily seat 300 parishioners. Its pews were draped in rustic velvet gold. The choir stand could hold up to 75 choir members. And the pulpit could seat six preachers comfortably. The church had a fellowship hall, family activity room, eight classrooms, and a board meeting room, two administrative offices and four bathrooms. The church was constructed with a white steeple that was in the form of a light house. The red and white brick of the church made it seem like a home away from home. On the top of the front doors it read, "New Light, where the light of God's love ever shines!" The Pastor's study was draped in carved wood and was equipped with a shower, a bathroom, a small kitchen area, a counseling room, a computer niche, and a small library. Lance's new office quarters spanned over 800 square feet. It reminded me of the hotel rooms that come equipped with a kitchen area. This was the nicest pastoral office space that Lance ever had. Upon his hire at New Light, we learned that the previous pastor requested that his office be remodeled and a member donated over $15,000 to honor his request. Oddly, enough four months after the renovations, the pastor resigned. Lance had yet to tell me the details of why the previous pastor resigned.

"What do you think of dear Sister Finley?" asked Lance as he looked into my eyes to watch the expression on my face.

"Well, she is friendly enough, a bit pushy, but she is okay. I guess."

"I hear that she is over 65 years old. But no one knows for sure," Lance said.

"No, she can't be! That lady doesn't look a day over 50!" I said.

"They say that she walks a mile a day, attends a day spa once a week and eats vegetables like they are going out of style. Her family inherited a lot of land in Southlake and made a fortune selling their land to incoming businesses. She's helped many businesses get on their feet and she has influence within the community as well. I heard her tell you that she is part of one of the founding families of New Light."

"Yes, she did."

"Well, New Light is just over 70 years old."

"Wow!"

"Her great grandfather was the founder of New Light and her grandfather was the next pastor after him. Her father probably would have been next in line to pastor New Light but he had a huge drinking problem that he just couldn't conquer, not even for the ministry."

"Babe, I pray that this time will be different for us," I said, while I turned to put my arms around his neck. I leaned toward him and laid my head upon his chest. I inhaled his Perry Ellis cologne, which seemed to mesmerize my senses. I knew that we were in a church, but I couldn't wait to get my man to our home, where it could be just the two of us.

"Hey, just listen and observe and don't be so quick to give your opinion or volunteer for anything just yet," said Lance as he gently raised my chin to look into my eyes.

"I've done that before, remember? Then I was called stuck-up and 'seemingly uninterested in God's work' as they said at Little Zion Church in their own words," I said with one hand on my hip. "And then when I did get involved, in the words of the members of Mt. Bethel, your first pastorage, 'I was overbearing and a little too opinionated,'" I said with a hint of bitterness.

"I know sweetheart, just be patient and try to feel them out first. Sister Finley certainly wants us to know who has been in charge in the interim, since they have been without a pastor for awhile."

"Speaking of their previous pastor, where is he now?"

"Well, the brother is no longer in the ministry. He and his wife are separated and the preacher's circles say he will probably be retiring from the ministry."

"Retiring! Isn't he only 53 years old?"

"Yes. But uh, let's just say he may have another child on the way, and it is not his wife's child, and he felt he needed to reevaluate his calling."

"Was she a member of this church, the other woman?"

"No. It is a woman he met during one of his annual revival trips. Apparently they have had an affair for over ten years. They have a seven-year-old and now another child on the way."

"How old is the other woman?"

"Well, she is old enough to know better. I heard that she is around 35 years old."

"Does the membership of New Light know about this scandal?"

"I'm not sure. The Deacons just found out the details late last month. They thought he just wanted to retire early and spend more time with his family. However, his wife found out about the 'other family' several months ago and she continually threatened to destroy him with the information, he felt he should probably retire and not have her blackmail him with his besetting sin. The sad thing though is that the man is a powerful pastor and teacher; however, he just had a weakness for this woman and never could get over it."

"Well, if he was such a powerful pastor and teacher he should have been able to learn from his own sermons and control his lusts and sinful temptations. Right?" I quipped.

"Oh no," Lance said rolling his head and letting go of our embrace.

I don't know why I tell you things like this because you go right on your pedestal about pastors being righteous men 24/7, but the reality is no one is righteous but God himself, we are just striving to be holy and working daily on righteousness. Really, the fact of the matter is that all men at times can be weak."

"Excuses, Excuses. Excuses are monuments of nothingness," I said.

In my heart, I secretly wondered if he had any "weak moments" during our marriage. Lord knows that some women in and outside of the church can be predators for men of the pulpit. Alright, Jacqueline, get off of your soapbox and change this subject quick.

"Lance, have you thought about your first sermon as pastor?" I asked.

"Now, sweetie, you know I rarely share my sermon titles before preaching," he said.

"Yes, I know, but not even a hint?" I questioned.

"Well, let's just say, Mission Possible: A Purpose Driven Church."

"Oh, sweetheart, that sounds interesting. Do you need help with the church programs for Sunday morning?"

"No, I have an interview scheduled for a new church administrative assistant."

"Oh, what happened to uh, what's her name, Mrs. Franklin?"

"The deacons determined that it is time to hire a new church assistant, Mrs. Franklin has been church assistant for 25 years, and she has not kept up with computer technology. Furthermore, she often sleeps at her desk. "

"How old is she?" I asked.

"Mrs. Franklin should be around 78 years old."

"Well then, I can fill in around the church until you hire a new assistant," I said.

"Sweetie, I don't think that is a good idea."

"Why not? This is a new city for me. I don't know the people well. The kids will soon be active in their school and extracurricular activities. I am accustomed to working with you in ministry."

"I know, baby, but let's take it slow. This is a huge opportunity for me and I don't want to be hasty about anything. You just rest and I'll take you out to dinner tonight, just you and I," Lance promised.

We walked out of the church arm in arm and he drove me back home and he returned to the church. I went upstairs to our bedroom and gathered the journal that has been a constant friend and a reminder of God's goodness. I opened my journal and began to read the testimonies of my life and the showcases of God's glory in our lives. An hour later, Lance arrived to take me to dinner.

For the last ten years I have kept a journal. I call my journal, *The First Lady: Joy for the Journey.* Over the years I have chronicled my family's ups and our downs. I have paper programs from our past churches, special days, special joys and testimonies enclosed in my journal. I have a prayer life map where God has answered our prayer requests. It will be my testimony for our descendants to discover the joy of serving Jesus. When I am writing, I am able to express my joy, my sorrow and even my pain. Often times, I address my journal notes to Jesus and other times, I write to the First lady when I need to pull off the coat of high expectations that dominate the life of a clergy wife. That night, I wrote about the newest experience in my Christian journey as a pastor's wife:

Dear Jesus,

It's 10:30 pm, the kids are in the bed, Lance got called to the hospital to visit an elderly member who had a sudden heart attack, as soon as we arrived at the restaurant. Bless his heart, he still stayed with me for 20 minutes to keep me company and I guess try to keep both the church and me (his two wives) happy. Oops, Lance constantly reminds me that I am his wife, and Jesus is the bridegroom that is talked about in the bible record of Revelation who will return for his church. As I watch Lance sleep, I thank You for his love for me and his family. He tries to be superman, but I am grateful Lord, that You gave him to me. He is not perfect, but he strives to be more like You. Jesus, as you already know, we are at a new church and new things abound for us. Protect us Jesus, like only you can. Help me find purpose in this church. Help me to be slow to speak and to love, unconditionally, the members of our church. Lord, finally I pray for my husband's strength during any "weak moments."

Love,

Jacqueline Renee Stevens, my confession

Chapter 2

A New & Improved Ministry

Well, it's been six months now and we have acquainted ourselves quite well with the New Light Church. It's Tuesday evening, and we're at church for choir rehearsals. Only 12 choir members remain in the choir after my husband decided to search for another worship leader and about 30 members left the choir in protest. Now they sit in the pews. One of the ex-choir members had the nerve to bring a newspaper to church and commenced to reading it when my husband mounted the pulpit last Sunday. Well, the previous musician, Brother Ray Joseph, never came to rehearsals or church on time. Worship services begin promptly at 11:00 am and he would stroll in at 11:15 and cause everything to be late. My husband counseled this young man many times, but he refused to follow my husband's leadership. Rumor has it that this young gentleman may have some sugar in his tank, if you know what I mean. When my husband asked him if he was a practicing homosexual he promptly responded no, rolled his eyes and strutted out the door. Now, I know that most male musicians in the church are typically stereotyped as being gay or the complete opposite; highly sexually charged, hence, a player, playa' just as some preachers' wives are stereotyped as being fat, materialistic, and supremely talented in the gift of music. Yet this young man, Brother Joseph, never attended bible study, he was pompous, he was not a continuous tither and he was constantly bragging about going to shady nightclubs in Dallas. Lord knows we should all love everyone regardless of their sin however, the male role model we display in front of our boys is important. My husband advised this young man that if he continued to not come to bible study or some form of church school and not tithe he would not continue to play at the New Light Church. Apparently this young man, had played at New Light since he was 15 years old. Oh, and it was a fiasco when he was officially fired in person and in the mail. He demanded that his uncle, Mr. Chambers, a respected deacon of the church, expel my husband from the pulpit because he was a dictator, without a heart for all of God's children. He was officially fired from being worship leader anyway and my husband encouraged him to remain a member of the church. Brother Joseph promptly refused. We haven't heard from him in the last two months.

So tonight is the night that my husband introduces the new Worship Leader and Coordinator. His name is Marcus Graves.

Brother Graves is a recent graduate of one of the nearby universities. He has been married for seven years and is the father of two young boys. He and his wife are both talented musicians and soloists in their own right.

My husband proudly announced, "Good Evening choir, I am excited about what God has in store for New Light's Music Ministry. I want you to meet Brother Marcus Graves, our new Worship Leader. This young man has come highly recommended and, most of all, he is saved and he loves Jesus. It is a pleasure to introduce New Light's New Worship Leader & Coordinator, Bro Marcus Graves."

As Marcus stood at his grand introduction, he looked at all the faces in the choir. Some of them smiled in return, others dared not look him in the eye, and others had the silently sarcastic question "What does he think he is going to do?"

Marcus exhaled. He opened up his first rehearsal with a prayer for the choir that past wounds and hurts would be healed with complete and total restoration for the choir. After the prayer, the eyes that seemed to avoid his eye, gave him a "He might just know what we need right now." He introduced his wife, Sister Juanita Graves, who slowly stood up as her husband spoke of her many musical gifts.

"This is my lovely wife of seven years, Sister Juanita Graves. She is a fine musician and soloist in her own right. But most of all she is a prayer warrior and trusted confidante. We are both grateful that God has led us to New Light and we intend to give the Lord our all in our service to Him. They made a handsome couple and their two small children were absolutely gorgeous.

Marcus Graves was 6'0 with chestnut brown skin and curly light brown hair which formed soft short trinkets around his face. He had a lean medium build, which illustrated that basketball might have been his favorite sport. Juanita was an ebony skinned, petite woman, no more than 5'2, and probably weighing 120 lbs in a wet rain coat. She possessed long cascading jet black curls which flowed to the middle of her back and a smile that could coo any little baby to sleep.

Sister Juanita Graves slowly looked around at the faces in the choir which seemed to say, "Whatever...so what if we care..." Juanita thought to herself, *Lord, we are going to need Your help.*

"Sweetheart, would you like to say anything?" asked Brother Graves.

Juanita shook her head, waved, and returned to her seat.

I thought to myself, "Girlfriend, you better get some guts or these people will eat you alive, first impressions are everything in the church. Lord, I'll need to start praying for her."

Pastor and I watched as Brother Graves worked his magic with the New Light choir. First, he listened to every voice in the choir and made necessary adjustments, such as switching a soprano to alto, a tenor to baritone, etc. This young man had skills in music and organization. The choir seemed mesmerized by his natural tenor voice and pianist skills. His wife accompanied him on the piano, while he played the organ.

This just might work. I looked at my husband; he winked his eye at me and smiled. Lord, I pray that my husband can finally get some peace. Lately, he'd been so restless due to all the talk surrounding why my husband fired Bro. Joseph. Let's just hope that everything will work out.

The following Sunday, the new and improved music ministry rocked the church house with Chester D.T. Baldwin's signature song, "God is Good." Brother Graves and Sister Graves were awesome with their new style of praise and worship which seemed to energize the young members in our church. They even introduced a new church theme song entitled, "The Light at New Light." My husband preached a sermon entitled, "Knocked Down, but Not Out!" and over four people joined church that Sunday. After six months at New

16

Light things were finally starting to come together. Thirteen people signed up that Sunday to attend the next choir rehearsal with the new musician team. There was a new energy and a new flavor of worship emerging at New Light and Lance and I began to rest in God's glory for all the new things He was doing within the church body.

Chapter 3

You Betta Watch & Pray

I looked at myself in the mirror and I'd gained 15 pounds since we've been here. My lord, who knows what I'll look like two years from now at the rate I'm gaining weight. Our one year Pastor & Family's appreciation service is in six months. I really don't want to walk down that aisle in a size 14-dress. What happened to me? Here, I am, looking like I feared I would be: A Pudgy Preacher's wife. Lance is a dear and he hasn't complained at all about my recent weight gain. Last week, we had three young, beautiful, and single women join our church and all the men, had to do a double take on one woman in the red suit, with matching hat, purse and shoes and hair down to her behind. I know she had to be sporting a 38-28-38 figure that she strutted down that aisle after giving her life to Christ. I heard that she works at Verizon or something like that. And to think, she is 34 years old and she has never been baptized or ever stepped into a church until she came to New Light. Her testimony in church last Sunday was a definite tear-jerker. People all over the church were crying and lifting up their hands in praise for God's power in bringing her to New Light.

Sister Peterson, the church mother and the oldest active member in the church, wrote me a note in church and scribbled, "First Lady, you betta' watch that woman in that red suit, she means us no good at New Light and you betta' pray. You betta' watch and pray!"

Sister Peterson is one of the oldest active members of our church at 79 years old. She is always writing notes in church and giving people warnings and advice. When I first came to New Light, I thought she was some type of voodoo woman because she always bragged about her mama's Louisiana roots and upbringing. She was known to walk into church with her beaded cane and purple feather hat. Since then, I have come to see her as somewhat of the church mother. Unfortunately, this wasn't the first time Sister Peterson had insinuated that I needed to watch that woman or this woman. Any time a halfway decent single woman under the age of 55 joined New Light, Ms Peterson would give me "the eye" which said "watch this one too." She had an old Southern traditional hymn that I called her code word hymn, if she was trying to give me a warning about another Sister in the church. Sister Peterson would walk by and sing:

> I don't know what Jesus is to you.
> But I hope He is to you what He is to me. He's my all, my all and all.
> He's my chief cornerstone.
> I don't know what Jesus is to you, but I hope he is to you-
> what He is to me.

If I heard Sister Peterson singing this song, sure enough there would be an attractive woman in the room. When we first arrived at New Light she used to scare my children to death singing that song all the time as she walked about doing her church work.

Sister Peterson had a time with "other women" when dealing with her late preacher husband, Pastor Henry Peterson. Personal experience can hinder anyone's fair judgment of people. As a result, Sister

Peterson is always "looking out" for her pastor's wife. She loves to tell me that just like some women are groupies around NFL or NBA bound men, there are women predators or groupies within the church who will stop at nothing to attract the wandering eye of a preacher. Well, that's Sister Peterson and all of her insecurities and her so called prophesies.

Sometimes though, it bothers me. All the junk she tries to bring me about other women in the church. I know that every woman in the church does not desire my husband. Truth be told, most are just attracted to my husband due to his favor from God. Think about it, have you even seen a knock out, drop dead gorgeous preacher/pastor? Yeah, there are not a lot of them out there that you would not want to look at twice. But it is their sensitivity and love for God that is attractive for most women. Lord knows if they knew what I know now, they might reconsider. Now don't get me wrong, I love my husband. I remember the first time we met in the University College Choir....

I walked in choir rehearsal wearing a pink silk blouse, black chiffon skirt and heeled pink sandals. My hair back then was light brown and cascaded midway down my back. I was boasting a trimmed down size eight and I felt and looked good. I wanted to make a good first impression with the choir music staff. I was so excited that the University of Texas had a gospel choir for its students. I had been singing gospel music in the church since I was three years old, when my first public solo was, "Oh, How I love Jesus." I was looking forward to meeting other college students who loved gospel music as much as I did. It was the initial rehearsal for the choir that year. And I walked into a room of over 50 African-American faces and I was so grateful to see others on campus that looked like me and I realized that I was home. Everyone was so nice and kind and welcomed all of the new freshman to rehearsal. We started singing and the choir director requested all of the sopranos to sing an A flat note. I belted out my customary soprano voice and the whole choir seemed to turn to me with a look on their faces that exclaimed, "Who is that?" In the midst of their faces, I noticed a dark mahogany colored brother in the tenor section, who gave me the sweetest smile from across the room, and nodded his head in a way that seemed to say, "Welcome." Toward the end of rehearsal, everyone introduced themselves.

And then it was my turn to introduce myself…

"Hello, my name is Jacqueline Montgomery and I am a freshman. My major is journalism with a minor in marketing. I am originally from Richmond, Texas. I graduated from Richmond High School. I am really happy to be here. I have been singing in the church since I was three years old and I know now that I have finally found some Christian friends here at the University of Texas who love gospel music just like I do.' I gave them my best smile and quickly took my seat.

And then it was his turn….

"Hello, and welcome to The University of Texas. My name is Lance McClain Stevens. I am a returning Junior. Yes, I made it through those first two years. Thank you Jesus! I am originally from Houston, Texas. I graduated from Jack Yates High School. I am currently majoring in Business with a minor in Philosophy. I am one of the newly elected choir directors of UT's Gospel Choir. We have great expectations for this choir not just musically but spiritually as well. Welcome to UT! Hook em' Horns!

And with that he sat down and gave me the sweetest smile from across the room. I was immediately uncomfortable and looked away from his gaze. A philosophy major, who is he fooling. I thought to myself. He must be preparing to preach. Lord knows, I don't want to be a preacher's wife.

After rehearsal, Lance found his way to the Soprano section, our eyes met and I made a dash to the door. Just as I was about to grab the doorknob, a short pudgy Alto crossed me off, "Hi, my name is Amanda Deshay. Welcome to UT. I noticed that you live across the hall from me. I'm a sophomore originally from Mt. Pleasant, right outside Tyler, Texas. Are you on your way back to the dorm?

"Uh, yes."

"Hey, let's walk together," Amanda volunteered.

"Excuse me, Ms. Montgomery."

I turned around and there he was with this big wide Denzel-like smile, Lance McClain Stevens.

"I noticed that you sing first Soprano quite well and we could really use your voice as one of our choir soloist and section leader. Our last Soprano section leader, graduated last year. What do you think?" he asked.

"Uh, well, I guess that'll be okay," I nervously answered. I don't know why I was so easily intimidated by this upperclassman. It must have been his broad shoulders, his 6'3 foot football player built frame and his cute deep dimples that caused me to feel so uncomfortable. Or perhaps it was his absolutely perfect pearly white teeth that caused my dizziness. I loved a man with a great set of beautiful white teeth. I thought I was about to faint for a moment.

"Great, our first rehearsal for the section leaders is this Thursday at 7pm in this same place. It was really nice meeting you," said Lance with a gleam in his eye.

He put out his hand and I gave him my hand. He had the strongest and firmest handshake. Lord knows I love a man with a firm handshake. My grandfather always told me a man with a firm handshake has character, inner strength and integrity.

Amanda and I watched him as he turned and walked away to meet with the other musicians and choir leaders.

"Girl, did you see the way he looked at you?" exclaimed Amanda as we walked toward our dormitory.

"Oh, he was just being nice," I said.

"Girl, you better recognize the difference between, nice and NICE...if you know what I mean. Lance Stevens has never looked at any girl in the choir the way he looked at you tonight. Girl, you just might be the next Mrs. Lance McClain Stevens."
"What do you mean?" I asked.

"I mean he has been too fixated on his music and his studies to even give any of the girls in the choir the time of day. That boy has seen some women obsess over him and he wouldn't even look at them twice. Have you heard him sing?"

"No," I said.

"Girl, the boy has a gospel Sam Cook sound. And he has range like gospel singers John P. Kee and Fred Hammond. Simply put the boy has mad singing skills."

"Then why is he majoring in business?" I asked.

"Well, he's a brainy guy too and he follows God's purpose for his life and right now it's to get an education."

"Sounds like you know a lot about him."

"Well, Lance is my second cousin. Our grandmothers were sisters. So yes, I do know a lot about him. During my freshman year, all of these junior and senior girls from the choir were trying to befriend me just to get closer to him."

"That must have been devastating."

"I received what I wanted out of my connection with Lance as well. I was instantly popular on campus because of my relationships with so many people. But, let me say, I haven't seen my cousin look at another female the way he looked at you tonight."

"Oh, well, I am not interested," I said looking away.

Amanda looked surprised.

"Oh, I get it, someone back home, yeah me too. But girl don't you want someone locally too? Why can't you have your cake and eat it too. The guys around here do it all the time."

"Well, I want to concentrate on my studies and I am not interested in dating a preacher."

"Oh, Lance is not preaching right now."

"Oh, he may not now, but he will be. I discerned that the moment he introduced himself. My purpose in life is not to be a church's first lady. I want to be my own woman and own my own Public Relations/Marketing Firm."

"Yeah, you are probably right about Lance. My grandmother said that he is just running from the pulpit. She said that Lance started preaching when he was two years old when he would mimic our old Pastor Barnes at our family's home church in Houston. They said Lance would spit, holler and wave his arms in a chicken dance when he was so called "preaching." And my grandma said Lance loved to go to church and would fall out if his grandmother didn't take him to Sunday school and church on Sunday. He did that from the age of two until he was five-years-old."

"He seems like a sweet person and I am sure we can be friends," I said.

"Well, you are now my new friend," Amanda said as we turned to enter our separate hall rooms.

"Listen if you need anything, just let me know."

"I will. Thanks Amanda for walking home with me," I said.

"Oh, girl its okay, we live in the same dorm so we might as well keep each other company."

"Okay, Amanda, you have a nice night. And let your cousin, Lance, know I said goodnight as well."

With that, she turned around with a gleam in her eye and said, "You can bet on that."

Chapter 4

A Time to Pray

It was the eve of dawning. The birds were chirping and the smell of spring was in the air. But something in the pit of my stomach let me know that something wasn't quite right. I arose out of bed, found my robe and headed to my prayer corner. I am so grateful that Lance is a man who believes in the power of prayer. After Lance called in a contractor to paint the parsonage a color I could live with, he had them build a nook and special alter that faced the window.

The house was quiet as I made my way to our place of prayer. Lance was in Austin preaching a three day revival. The children are in bed asleep waiting for the 6:00 am alarm to go off. A pang of sadness overwhelmed me. I am not sure where it came from, but I feel a sincere need to intercede for our church, and especially for my husband.

I fell on my knees in prayer.

> Dear God, the most High and Omnipotent. You are the Holiest of Holies. I adore your name, Jesus. I thank you for all of your blessings. I thank you for my family and the church that you have blessed us with. Lord, I come interceding for

my precious husband. Lord, protect him from all hurt and danger. Keep him in your loving arms. Keep him humble, Oh God. Speak to him so that he may speak to your people. Cleanse him from any sin and restore his spirit. Give him the Joy of your salvation. Watch over our babies and show them your way; direct them and guide them. Lord, I pray for the sick in our church; the spiritually sick and the physically sick. Give us all a hunger for your word and a desire to do your will. Watch over, New Light and every church that stands open in your name. Let us all possess a kingdom building spirit to overtake the world for Christ. And finally lord, please Lord, I pray that Sister Mary Temple will one day be restored to her right mind and her trust in YOU completely restored. I praise you Jesus for all that you have done for our family, our church, and our friends; In Jesus' holy name, amen.

I always pray for Mary Temple. A pastor's wife I met just five years earlier at a Ministers' Wives Conference in Houston, TX. Mary was a brilliant speaker at the conference. She testified about her 15 years as a senior pastor's wife with a 2,000 plus member congregation. She was a marvelous speaker who testified about her Christian journey in the role of a minister's wife. She shared her mistakes, her bitterness, her anger and then her joy. Mary was now seeing a psychiatrist after suffering an exhaustion breakdown two years ago. After 18 years of marriage, she discovered her husband was having an affair with a fellow male parishioner for the last five years and that he suffered from sexual addiction; thus engaging in sex with both men and women. Mary was devastated and humiliated as news of her husband's indecent affairs became public knowledge. Her marriage was hit a devastating blow and they watched as the church membership fell to under 100 members in just eight short months. Everything she seemed to have sacrificed for had been stripped away by a total confession from her husband. He confessed that he had a life-threatening sexually transmitted disease. Her husband died just three years ago with Mary by his side. She forgave her husband, but unfortunately she failed to address her own emotional and mental needs, so one day her mind just shattered.

"Lord, I wonder if I would be able to handle everything she had to go through," I said out loud. My heart still aches for Mary Temple. At that moment, my spirit longed for my husband to return by my side. I miss him so much when he is gone. I walked to the phone to dial his hotel number.

"Hello," he said with a groggy voice.

"Hey, babe, I just wanted to hear your voice," I said.

"How were services last night?" I asked.

"We had a great time. The Holy Spirit was in the place. What time is it?"

"It's about 5:45 am. I'm sorry to call you so early, but I miss you when you are gone." I paused to measure my next words. "Is everything ok, sweetie? I woke up with a strong urge to pray for you this morning."

"Did you pray for me?" Lance asked.

"Of course, sweetie. Is everything ok?"

"I got a phone call from the chairman, Deacon Jenkins late last night. We're going to have a meeting within the next couple of weeks."

"What about?" I asked.

"I am not too sure, but it may have to do with our former musician. I heard that he has been trying to sabotage me with the ministers in the area and he is making accusations against me."

"Accusations?! That boy hardly knows you! What kind of accusations?"

"Honey, we'll talk about it when I return. I really don't want to focus on that while I am trying to focus on the message for this revival. I don't want Satan to distract me."

"I know, baby."

"What food do you want me to prepare for you when you come home?" I asked.

"I will probably go with Pastor West and some of the other preachers to dinner Thursday night. But I will look forward to breakfast in bed with you, Goldie."

I love it when he calls me Goldie!

"Alright, babe, you got it! Should I have the honey ready?" I asked in my sexy whispering voice.

"Yes, Yes, get it ready for me!"

I love that we still have the passion to satisfy one another in more ways than one.

"I love you, baby," I said.

"I love you too, Goldie. Give my children a big hug from their daddy and let Junior know I will be at his game on Friday. That is a promise!"

"Okay, get some rest, bye."

I hung up the phone and sighed, grateful that my husband loved me and his family. Thank you, God for waking me up to say a prayer for him. I knew something wasn't quite right. Over the years, as a wife and mother, I have learned to pray for my husband and my family. I believe it is something that God gives the Christian woman, to be in tune with her family. It is the still small voice or the gut feeling of a woman's instinct to guard and protect her family. My Bigmama Thompson always said that if I could not sleep at night, then God was waking me up to pray and ask Him to cover my situations, family, and friends with prayer. I remember as a little girl, waking up to my grandmother's sing-song prayers. "Lord, bless my family, keep us together, make us strong and bold for your glory." Yes, my Bigmama, Johnnie Mae Thompson, can pray and I love hearing her talk to her God.

My Bigmama T, as her grandchildren affectionately call her, taught me to strive for my dreams and keep God first in my life. Bigmama T is a go-getter. She and Bigdaddy owned two restaurants and the first black nursing home in the small city of Richmond, TX. They had over 30 rent houses and were very active in local politics and the church. They were also financial lenders to the black community, loaning money and charging 35 % interest. Yes, you heard me right, 35% interest!! Bigmama T said she charged 35% because it was to discourage everybody from seeking a loan from them. They typically loaned money only for emergencies when the family could not get a loan from the local white-owned bank or from family members. But she prided herself in loaning her people money because she gave them up to five years to pay her back.

My maternal grandparents did very well for themselves. Yet it wasn't their houses and land that impressed me; it was their devotion to prayer, God and his church. My Bigdaddy only had a sixth grade education and he couldn't read very well. So every week, I had to read the Sunday school lesson to him and he would memorize the words so that he could teach it on Sunday. He was the chairman of the deacon board and the Sunday School Superintendent. Very few of the church folks knew that he couldn't read that well. However, reading the Bible and the Sunday school lessons for my Bigdaddy gave me a love for God's Word.

My parents lived across town in Richmond, TX on family inherited land called Montgomery Quarters. It was family legacy that my paternal great-great-great grandfather was a famous southern carpenter and he saved his monies from his work to buy over 100 acres of land that he divided up among his family members. He named this acreage "Montgomery Quarters." And for over 75 years the Montgomery Descendants lived and retired on this land. In the 1970s my great-uncle Robert Montgomery, who was an architect, redeveloped the land and developed a 50-house plot subdivision which was aptly named Montgomery Estates. Each house sat on at least three acres of land, complete with at least four bedrooms in each house, sidewalks, curbed streets, three parks, and a recreation center. This is where my parents built their dream home while I was still in high school. Frankly, I thought our five bedroom farm house on ten acres was a great place, but my Daddy agreed to let Uncle Robert redevelop our land and make it a part of Montgomery Estates so Uncle Robert turned it into a seven bedroom, four bathroom, and three car garage with beautiful green landscaping paradise. I still remember my mother's face when our new home was complete. A small tear of joy fell from her face, as my mother looked at me and said, "One day, this will be yours. This is our family legacy. Our family's sweat, tears and hard work define this land. Never forget the sacrifice." I was the oldest of three girls and my mother was always talking to me about taking care of my younger sisters and honoring the family legacy of land and prosperity.

So you can imagine her disappointment when I married a smart, intelligent, working class preacher. My mother was Eva Montgomery, wife of attorney John Montgomery and daughter to Edward and Johnnie Mae Thompson. Both affiliations gave her great pride and she was considered to be a blessed woman of prosperity in our small town of Richmond. Eva wanted nothing but the best for her three daughters. My mother was a woman who loved the Lord, but I wondered if she just attended church because it was considered to be a "proper" thing for women of prestige. Going to church in the South was an unspoken rule for most women of money, black or white. I still recall an article in Jet Magazine I saw my mother reading that said most middle class people attend church. She remarked after completing the article, "If our people in the ghettos would just attend church, it just may take them out of poverty. But they would rather wait for their monthly government check. It's so sad, so sad." Well, that was my mama. She attended our local family church Mt. Moriah Church, founded by my maternal great, great uncle. My mom was a deaconess, a youth matron, member of the Local Links Chapter, charter member of the local Jack-N-Jill,

33

charter member of Delta Sigma Theta Sorority in Richmond and a graduate of Texas Southern University where she obtained her B.S. and Masters in education in the 1960's. She married John Montgomery, then a law student at Texas Southern University and heir to vast land in the Montgomery Quarters in Richmond. I absolutely adored my daddy. He was the balance that our family needed. He was quiet, strong and humble. He loved his Montgomery daughters. He taught us strength, ambition and the love of Jesus. In the eyes of our father, his daughters could do no wrong. However, if we did, he was a strong disciplinarian who taught us about hard work and efficiency. He would work us like boys on the farm, he taught us how to change a tire on a car and unclog a sink drain, and then my daddy would cuddle his girls like his little darlings. John Montgomery was a bear in the courtroom. He was one of the few black attorneys in the local Richmond area. Furthermore, Houston area judges and attorneys of all nationalities respected him.

He served as a deacon at Mt. Moriah. I believe he ran from his calling as a minister due to my mama's absolute objections to being a minister's wife. She truly did not want to be called a minister's wife and experience all of the restrictions that came along with it. I would hear my parents argue many times about my daddy's desire to preach and my mama telling him that he was doing fine as just a deacon in the church. She was afraid of the pulpit and its demands. Besides, she felt like he had more control in the church as a deacon. She loved my daddy so much that she didn't want to share him with anyone, especially not any of the sisters in Richmond, who eyed her husband every Sunday. She did not want to leave their precious land if daddy were given a call to pastor a church in a new city. She loved her life in Richmond. Daddy died of a heart attack at age 56. I was totally devastated. I rushed home from our small church in Cypress, TX to be by my daddy's side as he whispered his last breaths.

He died in my mother's arms as she sang, "Yes, Jesus loves you." We had to make the difficult decision to remove him from life support as the doctors told us that he was legally brain dead. It seemed as if my whole world was falling apart. My daddy, my strength, the one who made me laugh, who held me in his arms and said everything would be okay, was gone.

He died two years after Lance received the call to pastor a small church in Cypress, TX. named Mt. Bethel Church. His pastorate only lasted four years; he resigned due to the deacon board's desire to tell him what to preach and what not to preach. Their wives refused to speak to me and pretty much acted like I didn't even exist. That is, until my son spilled some crackers on their beloved carpeted church floors. I'll never forget that Sunday morning, Sister Newsome noticed that my eight-month-old son, who was teething at the time, dropped some crackers on the floor and she got all in my face, "Its people like you who give the saints of God so much to worry about. Did you not see your baby dropping these crumbs on the floor? Are you blind, Sister Stevens? I don't care if he is a baby, thou shall not eat in the Holy Sanctuary of the Most High God! And that goes for your baby too! You are supposed to be setting a good example for the young women of Mt. Bethel, but instead you don't have any respect for our God and to think He chose you to be a minister's wife!" As she screamed, spit from her crazy verbal rampage landed on my dress.

I chose not to respond. I grabbed my baby, my bible, politely smiled, rolled my eyes, turned my heels and walked away. You know it is those legalistic Christians who will be sour about not receiving any rewards when they get to Heaven due to how they treated others. Sister Newsome never asked me how my baby was doing, neither did she know that he was having a terrible time teething and was on medication to relieve his pain. All she saw were the crackers on the floor. It was just a crazy situation and I was grateful to God when Lance resigned from Mt. Bethel and we moved to Tyler, TX. to pastor Little Mt. Zion Church for eight and a half years.

Reflections

Lord, you have brought us a mighty long way and you have protected us throughout the entire process. Yes, Jesus, you have been good to us in spite of what others may have done or said to us. I stayed on my knees as I looked out of the window of our prayer nook and tears of joy fell gently down my face. Thank you, God for joy in this journey.

Chapter 5

Traditions

It was early first Sunday morning on a beautiful spring Texas day. New Light Fellowship Hall was littered with the early bird saints who arrived at 6:45am for prayer, coffee and conversation. This tradition of the deacons, ministers and their wives meeting in the early Sunday morning started at New Light over 50 years ago as the leaders of the church would meet to fellowship and start planning for morning worship. It was during this time that the deacons and ministers would sit at the table, drink coffee, and talk about community happenings and plans for the church. This fellowship time was equivalent to businessmen who met on the golf course to secure their business dealings and ventures. This was also a time where the deacons' and ministers' wives would fellowship and spend time encouraging one another. This particular Sunday morning, Sister Peterson arrived at 6:45 am on the dot with her beige winter hat, beige matching cane and purse and a winter white pearl lace dress that fell to her ankles. The only thing that spoke to Sister Peterson's beginning dementia were her white stockings and red sandal shoes that she wore with this outfit.

"Good morning, Sister Stevens" said Sister Peterson. "I haven't seen you at the morning gathering for quite some time."

"Good morning, Sister. The children stayed at the Caldwell's last night, so I am able to come and join the fellowship this morning. How are you feeling, Sister Peterson?" I asked.

"The Good Lawd has blessed me to see another Sunday morning! And Oh how precious it is, chile. I will be 80 years old on December 18th and I praise God for every new day! Hallelujah! "

"I am grateful too, Sister Peterson, for a new morning that I have never seen before," I said.

Sister Peterson sat her lean 130lbs frame down at the table, kindly placing her cane and bible by her side. It was a quiet in the fellowship hall as Sister Peterson looked around to see who was around us.

"Sister Stevens," said Sister Peterson.

"Yes," I replied.

"Why do you let these folks call you First Lady? You know when my husband was pastoring he told me that I wasn't the First Lady. He was adamant that the church was his first lady and so he outright would denounce that saying and I didn't like it either and would tell off any member that called me First Lady."

"I guess I just consider it a term of endearment. You know, it's a phrase of respect. It doesn't hurt my feelings when they call me that, Sister Peterson. At first, I didn't embrace it, but I don't hinder anyone from calling me that now. I see it as the same type of respect that preachers give each other when they call each other "Doc." Now you and I both know that a lot of black preachers with

"Dr." in front of their name haven't completed any type of accredited doctoral program. So the term "first lady" is also equivalent to the fact that we call preachers Reverend as a term of endearment or a sign of respect. The exact word reverend is not even mentioned in the bible when speaking concerning ministers, preachers, elders, but it is a word that was developed by men taken from the word reverence as a token of respect because, we are to respect and give double honor to the man of God. Therefore, the terms, First lady and Reverend are terms of respect and endearment."

"Hmm. Chile, it seems like you did your homework on that. Well, I have to confess. I told some members to stop calling you First Lady because you weren't anybody's first lady. You were a member just like the rest of us."

"I am a member, Sister Peterson. I come to church, participate and pay my tithes just like you do," I said.

"I know. I guess I'm just stuck in tradition that's all," said Sister Peterson.

"Don't worry, it is not a salvation issue," I said with a smile.

"I remember all the sacrifices I made for our church. My Henry put everything before his family. He truly believed that the church came before his family. He put the church, his money and his women before us. You know I can't be upset that two of our six children have not set foot in a church in over 20 years. They resented the church for taking their daddy away from them. Your husband preached a sermon just two months ago about prioritizing in your Christian journey. He called that sermon, "The Right Order." I recall him saying that its: God, family and church in that order. If only my

Henry would have had that type of order in his life. Sometimes, I think the man married me, just so he could pastor a church."

"Oh, Sister Peterson, don't say that," I said.

"It's probably true. We were married over 40 years and he never really let me in his heart until his last few years. He loved the church so much. She was his first lady. Yeah, his first lady...He let the women in the church just treat me any kind of way. You know, I had a fight on the church steps with one of his women!"

"Sister Peterson, you have got to be kidding?"

"Naw, chile. I whooped that woman up something good. She came flaunting up to me and whispered in my ear, 'He was sure good last night.' Before I knew it, I whacked that heifer with my purse and my bible. It took three deacons to get me off of her. My Henry just stayed in his office the next two hours, too embarrassed to preach that morning. The poor fool had to pick me up from jail after church that evening. All he kept saying was that he was so sorry. One time he even had the nerve to tell me that he had a three-week revival in upstate New York. Baby, by this time we were married for about 25 years and I was sick of the lies and his games. I had never flown on an airplane before, but I bought a ticket and flew to his so called three-week revival," said Sister Peterson.

"Well, was your Henry at a revival?" I asked.

"That was one time I caught him at his game. He did have a revival. It was a four-day revival. But I caught him with a 23-year-old gal just living the life in the summertime of upper New York. You would have thought the man had a heart attack when he saw me walking up to him on that beach."

"What made me you stay by his side?" I quizzed Sister Peterson.

"You see the man loved his church so much, that he was afraid that I would let the church members know. I hired a private investigator to take pictures of him and his woman before I caught him red handed on that beach. And so I played my own game. I told him I wanted to become a full-time housewife and retire. At the time I was working two jobs as a teacher and an after school counselor to send our babies to college. I made him promise to send all of our children to the college or trade school of their choice and that I could quit my jobs to support him in ministry or else those photos would find their way to his beloved church deacon board."

"Oh no, you didn't Sister Peterson!" I said with a hearty laugh.

"Yes I did, I was too old and I wasn't trying to find another man, so I could train him too. I just made that preacher man of mine do right by me because he had a greater love for the church, not God, but he loved the adoration that the church gave him and he put them before God and his family. So honey, if I sometimes sound like a bitter woman, I probably am at times. I am praying that God takes this bitterness away from me completely. I know what Proverbs says about bitterness in 17:22 "A merry heart does good like medicine, but a broken spirit dries the bones." So I am learning to have a merry heart in spite of what has occurred in my life, because I don't want these bones of mine to become brittle and my heart cold. I learned to forgive my Henry with a merry heart. You know I have cooled down some. I didn't trust any woman with an hourglass figure and bone straight hair that walked in our church. I know that was like a jealous woman scorned and a sin in God's eye to just judge any woman like I did. But I just didn't trust my Henry around any good-looking woman. They just made that man weak in the knees. Well, everyone has a weakness, including our preacher men. My Henry once said that a sermon should be just like a skirt, long enough to cover the most important stuff and short enough to still be interesting. Yes, indeed, my Henry loved to chase after them skirts," chuckled Sister Peterson.

"Excuse me for asking, Sister Peterson, but what happened to him?"

"Ten years ago, he died of a prostate cancer at the age of 72. You know he was player in his day, but the last 12 years of his life, that man was completely loyal to me. He retired from the church at the age of 65 and I think Godly wisdom taught him the error of his ways. All of our children have professional degrees, thanks to their daddy's promise to send them to college and three of them are active in their church and community."

I often wondered why Sister Peterson came to church alone so I was surprised to learn that she had so many children.

"Where are your children now, Sister Peterson?" I asked.

"My oldest boy lives in New York City. He is an accountant and a minister. He has two children. The rest of my children live in Atlanta, Georgia. One is an attorney, the other a college professor, and two of them are engineers. My baby boy is a pastor in Decatur, Georgia. We are all so proud of him. All together they have given me 12 beautiful grandchildren and 2 great grandchildren. Yes, chile the Lord blessed me with my family!" My Henry would be so proud of his children."

"What brought you to Texas, Sister Peterson?"

"Why this is my father's family's home, I inherited a house from my paternal grandmother in Southlake. Henry and I retired here after he retired from the church. He promised me that we would move to northeast Texas and spend our last days together."

"Do you think Mr. Henry loved you?" I carefully quipped.

"I think Henry learned to love me. I don't know if it was that, or the onset of prostate cancer he developed that actually slowed his playing days down. You know this time was before the days of Viagra," laughed Sister Peterson.

"I don't think his motivations were pure when we first married, but the good Lord, after many years, turned Henry's heart toward me. I think it's because I always prayed that God would grant me favor and give Henry a genuine love for me. So in our old age, he fell in love with me for the first time."

"Sister Peterson, that is a beautiful story, at times sad, but eventually victorious!!"

"God knows what he is doing," said Sister Peterson, grabbing her cane while looking around to see the young children coming into the fellowship hall to start their Sunday school class. Sister Peterson wobbled her way up to a stance.

With a sparkle in her eye and a wink, Sister Peterson said, "I guess its time for us to stop talking and prepare to learn about the Lord. Come on, First Lady, and let's get ready for class."

I looked at her when she called me First Lady. It was a term she never used to refer to me. However, her wink let me know that she had shared something special with me. She had opened up her chest of treasures and allowed me to look inside her past history to help me understand the Sister Peterson she is today. I watched as this nostalgic 79 year old woman made her way to her Sunday school class and I then admired her dedication to God to serve Him in spite of her own disappointments and pitfalls in her life.

Then without missing a beat Sister Peterson turned around and said, "And First Lady, you still got to watch them young women after your husband. Treat your husband like a King and he will treat you like the Queen. They don't necessarily want your husband they just want the favor that God has on his life. Pray for your husband that he won't be weak in the knees for those young thangs like my Henry. But then if those sisters mess with ya' just give em' one good left hook, that'll teach them to leave ya' alone."

"Yes Maam," I replied. I grabbed my bible and purse and joined her walking toward the Adult Women's Sunday school class. I thought to myself, this woman is still somewhat crazy and thinks that every woman is after the preacher man. It was sad that in her old age she characterized every single woman in the church under the age of 55 as a roaming predator of married preacher men. I shook my head and smiled as the image of Sister Peterson fighting a woman on the church steps entered my mind. If dementia did take her good mind, she still did have her fighting spirit and a good left hook.

Chapter 6

The Beauty Shop Experience

Upon relocating to northeast Texas, I loved and at times I hated going to Vivian's Heavenly Hands Beauty Salon. This was a place where the women of Southlake gathered together for the community gossip and often times the people and the good church folks of Southlake were the top discussions. I really think that it often turned to church because of Vivian's bitterness over the church. You see, Vivian Daniels, who was the owner and operator of Heavenly Hands was an accomplished organist who had played at various churches within the county since the age of 12. However, she and her then Pastor had a disagreement and she left the church for good. She hadn't played a church organ in over ten years. At the age of 47, Vivian lived a carefree life free of the demand of playing in church Sunday after Sunday. She traveled extensively and loved to watch those televangelists who taught prosperity and finance. Vivian believed in the principle of prosperity so much that it led her to the Louisiana Casinos and the Houston Horse tracks on a monthly basis. So naturally, she loved when folks came into the shop with their share of church news. Vivian was known for her expensive taste and her salon was always decorated to a tee. Every three months she changed the color scheme of her salon. Today it was decorated in pink and green. Ms. Vivian loved to pamper her customers so today she catered from her cousin Thelma

Henderson's restaurant, fried catfish and shrimp for her afternoon customers.

I walked in the salon to see Ms. Vivian's tall 5'9, voluptuous frame walk elegantly toward me to give me her trademark bear hug which was the customary greeting for all of her customers. Ms. Vivian could have easily been a model with her oval mahogany shaped face and her lean but strong frame. She was wearing long golden micro braids in a Japanese twist up do. Her spring green linen dress and matching green sandals were a great accent to her recently redecorated pink and green salon draperies and accessories.

"Good evening, Sister Stevens, how are you doing?" asked Vivian.

"I am doing fine, Ms. Vivian," I said.

"How is the Preacher and those beautiful children?" she asked.

"The Lord is blessing us. I love your pink and green decorations this quarter."

I noticed a pink and green elephant on the salon shelf and I thought to myself, if my Mother Dear who was a faithful member of Delta Sigma Theta were to see this pink and green elephant she would proudly faint.

"Sister Stevens, what can I do for you today?" asked Ms. Vivian.

"I think I need a perm and I'll take one of your classic Ms. Vivian French rolls."

People from as far away as 100 miles came to Ms. Vivian's Heavenly Hands to receive one of her signature French Rolls. Lance loved when I had my hair in one of these up does. He said that Ms. Vivian's French Rolls made me look like a princess. So I thought that I would get a nice up do for his return on Thursday night and make our Friday morning even more romantic. I had already requested off from work on Friday to spend the day with Lance. I made an appointment for him at our local Total Wellness Spa to receive a massage and a pedicure. I pray nothing interrupts this appointment for Lance. I constantly encourage him to take care of himself physically or I will be a widow at 50 years old if he didn't learn to relax and pamper himself.

Interrupting my thoughts, Vivian said, "Come have a seat. I am ready for you now. So how is the great New Light Church?" she asked in her customary sarcastic tone.

I walked over to the salon chair and sat down while Vivian began to brush my hair and spray some soft sheen on my scalp to prepare for the application of my relaxer.

"The church is doing fine. The Lord is blessing us," I replied.

I had learned early in the days of being a Pastor's wife that people loved to "pick" the Pastor's wife to find out if certain rumors or gossip being circulated were true. For some reason, preachers' wives were automatically deemed credible as if they had a 411 on the truth of a matter.

"I heard that you all got rid of your former musician and the Lord has blessed you with a dynamic duo in Marcus and Juanita Graves," said Vivian.

"Yes, the Lord has blessed us with a great musical team in the Graves," I said, purposefully not trying to answer the first comment about our former musician. I had learned that short and sweet responses were key to getting persons to feel uncomfortable enough to eventually change a subject.

Ms. Vivian looked at Sister Stevens and thought to herself, she is a good one. She never says more than she is supposed to unlike Pastor Wiley's new wife, the third Sister Wiley in the last 20 years. Sister Patricia Wiley, at 31 years of age, seemed to resent the demands and the fishbowl experience of being a preacher's wife and every week she came into Heavenly Hands and gave her own brand of church gossip and her own hurts within the church. Sister Wiley fell for every "pick" that Vivian and her local customers asked of her. But Sister Stevens was a seasoned preacher's wife who understood credibility and the art of being discreet. Vivian had to admit that she admired and respected Sister Stevens for her discretion in protecting her family and her church.

"Have you talked to Sister Wiley lately?" Vivian asked.

"I haven't seen or spoken to Sister Wiley in over two months," I carefully responded.

I thought to myself and I probably won't be speaking to her any time soon after I sat her down and cautioned her about her tongue. Two months ago, Sister Wiley came to the salon to drop off some money she owed to Vivian and she stayed over an hour gossiping about the women and the deacons in her husband's church. The poor girl fell for every question they asked her and then some information she volunteered for free. After Sister Wiley left the salon,

Ms. Vivian said, "Now there is a preacher's wife who talks entirely too much." And they all laughed at her when they thought I was under the hair dryer but they didn't realize my dryer had turned off and I heard their entire conversation about Sister Wiley. I called Sister Wiley and cautioned her about sharing too much inside information and shared a verse in Proverbs 17:28 Even a fool is thought wise if he keeps silent, and discerning if he holds his tongue.

She listened to me but I think she resented me for giving her any counsel, so she hasn't called or dropped by the salon on my customary salon days. Sister Wiley had only been a pastor's wife for eighteen months so she was presently being schooled on the do's and the don'ts of the First Lady Sorority. This was her first marriage and she was still learning how to be a good wife. Pastor Wiley married her after his second wife died of a massive stroke. It was the talk of Southlake when Pastor Wiley age 58, married a 29 year old young nightclub singer by the name of Patricia Carry. After they married, Pastor Wiley baptized her and welcomed her into his church as his new bride, Sister Patricia Carry Wiley. I still don't understand why some pastors marry women who do not know the Lord. Then when their wife acts a fool, and does things and says things uncustomary to the church, the pastor wonders why. For instance, one time, Sister Wiley actually told a customer in the salon that she knew for a fact that Pastor Wiley had affairs on the former, now deceased second Sister Wiley, and the first Sister Wiley who died giving birth to their first son. I looked at her and wondered to myself, "Why on earth would she share that information with anyone. Was she trying to ruin her husband?" Personally, I believe she liked the attention of being a somewhat automatic, credible representative because she was now a Pastor's wife. Either that or Sister Wiley was just young, stupid, and naïve about people's motivations and sincerity. If she was ever to experience joy in the journey of being a minister's wife she would have to learn to control her tongue and pray for wisdom to discern others true motivations.

"I hear that old man Wiley and his new young wife may be on the rocks right now. She came in here yesterday complaining that she wants to have a baby and the old man told her that he was done having babies with anyone. She was just crying in front of everybody because she desires to be a mother. I could hardly complete her hair because she was crying so hard. My customers just looked at me like, 'something is not right with this woman.' They all looked at her like she was a manic-depressive or something. Some days she comes in the salon on a high and other times she is downright depressed and bawling all over the place," said Vivian.

Ms. Vivian was known to over exaggerate a situation so I knew that Sister Wiley had come in here and needed a place to vent her frustrations so she choose the salon and she might have only cried once.

"Has she cried in here before, Ms. Vivian?"

"No, that was the first time she broke down like that. It really made my customers uncomfortable so I finished her hair and led her to my back office where she slept for a few hours and then I called Pastor Wiley to come and pick her up. He looked so embarrassed when he walked in and had to lead his weeping wife out of a salon filled with at least three women from his church watching him. So you know it was the talk at their church that next Sunday. By the way, what is the name of their church?"

I knew Ms. Vivian knew the name of the church; she was trying to coax me to comment to her remarks.

"I believe its Mt. Olivet Church," I replied and hastily ended my comment. After about two minutes of silence Ms. Vivian said, "Yes, it is Mt. Olivet Church."

Oh, well thought Ms. Vivian, so much for getting Sister Stevens to talk. I even left her lye perm on her hair a little longer to see if she would talk about Sister Wiley.

"Okay Sister Stevens, let's go to the shampoo chair and wash this relaxer out of your hair," said Vivian.

Thank God! I thought to myself, I thought the woman was going to burn my hair off with that lye perm! She was just trying to get me to talk about some mess and I had crossed my legs the entire time to not focus on the pain of the lye perm she was applying to my hair or her silence to get me to talk. My worst nightmare was an atomic bomb or catastrophic explosion occurring during a time when I was receiving a lye perm in a beauty salon!

After Ms. Vivian washed, dried, and styled my hair into her signature French roll. I made an appointment with her receptionist within the next two weeks. I went into the salon women's bathroom, looked at my hair and freshened up my makeup. I looked at the mirror and thought I don't look bad for a 38 year old woman. My sweetheart is going to love my hair. Now if I just lose these last 15 lbs on my waistline. Lord, can you please help me lose this weight?

I adjusted my clothes, walked out of the restroom, said my customary good-byes to the other patrons in the salon and issued my monthly invitation to Ms. Vivian to come and visit New Light.

"Ms. Vivian, we would love for you to visit New Light. You have been promising me that you would visit. I have lived here now almost a year and you have yet to visit. I tell you what; I am personally inviting you to our 1st Pastor's & Family Appreciation Sunday in two weeks."

"Sister Stevens, I am going to check my calendar and I will see if I can make it. I am not promising you anything but I will see. Are you coming that week to get your hair done as well?"

"Yes. I made an appointment with your receptionist," I replied.

"Now, will you be wearing the customary Preacher's wife hat? So that means you will get a wash and set that week, right?" Ms. Vivian asked.

I looked around the salon, immediately feeling a little uncomfortable as all eyes were now on me.

"I am really not sure what I will be wearing just yet, but when I do know I will call you."

I hated that people felt that all preacher wives needed to wear a hat on the Appreciation Day. I truly liked wearing church hats. My paternal grandmother, Anna Belle Montgomery introduced me to church hats when I was just 14 years old. I paraded in church hats long before I married a preacher. My Granny Montgomery had a church hat that cost over $2,000 and she let me wear it in a most beautiful hat contest held at our church in Richmond when I was 16 years old. I won the coveted award for "Most Stylish Hat." Granny Montgomery just winked at me when I won, because no one in the church even recognized that it was her hat. She had always told me that I looked beautiful in a church hat and that only a certain kind of woman knew how to strut in a church hat. I remember practicing my walk with her church hat on my head. Some of her hats were wide brimmed, while others were coifed and short. Whatever the occasion, Granny Montgomery had a church hat to match. My daddy once said she spent an average of $10,000 a year on purchasing church hats and matching shoes and purses. When Granny Montgomery died she willed her church hats to me. So I have a stash of over 100 church hats in our outside storage house. As a result, some people have often referred to me as "The Hat Lady." I have chosen not to join the choir at New Light so I am able to really sport my church hats a lot more than I used to.

"Well ladies, I will see you in about two weeks. Thanks Ms. Vivian. I love my hair."

"Yes, it is beautiful on you, Sister Stevens. Tell the family I said hello and I'll see you before the big day. You have a good night."

"Good night, Sister Stevens," echoed the other patrons who were being serviced by Ms. Vivian's other hair operators.

"You too," I replied. I knew the moment I walked out of the shop my name could possibly be the center of their next discussion.

Chapter 7

A Wounded Soul and a Bitter Cup

As soon as Sister Stevens exited the front door of Heavenly Hands, the ladies began their discussion concerning the preacher's wife, Sister Stevens.

"Now Vivian, you know that Sister Stevens knows what she is going to wear to her husband's appreciation service. I don't know why you play with her like that," said Mrs. Woodard, a 50-year-old something church deaconess at Rose of Sharon Church who was sitting down in a chair receiving a roller set.

"I wasn't playing with her. I may have been out of the church for a while, but I do know that the First Lady is expected to wear a hat on appreciation day," replied Vivian.

"Now, Viv, why should she wear a hat?" asked Mrs. Woodard.

"Hey, I don't know, you church folks make up all the rules. You know church school on Sunday at 9:30am, Worship at 11:00am. You can't wear pants in the church, women are to shut up, don't preach and don't talk, but you can play our piano and cook us dinners. Now, why does church school have to be on Sunday morning? You know that big mega church down the highway that has over 4,000 members? I heard they have Church School during the week and Worship Services only on Wednesdays and they have a seeker service or something like that on Sundays, just for the sinner folks. And they don't have all of these 3:30pm afternoon services and 6pm Sunday evening services that are nearly empty. They are in to do one thing, worship God and then they are out. And that is why they are growing at the seams right now. They are not stuck in tradition like folks in our community. So honey, I didn't make the rules, those old nasty men made the rules and one rule is that the First Lady is to look like a classy lady and wear a hat. I wonder what color Sister Stevens will be wearing? I may have to help her dress up and find a dress for her, because she is a little plain and it looks like she has gained some weight too."

All of the women and the three hair operators in the shop laughed except Mrs. Woodard.

"Viv, have you joined that big church up the highway since you like them so much?" asked Mrs. Woodard.

"No, I just don't like their song service; it's a little too boring for my taste. You know I have to have my gospel singing, that good old gospel singing. So I haven't found that kind of church with the flavor that I am looking for."

Mrs. Woodard knew that after ten years of being away from the church, Ms. Vivian would find a way to keep from going back to church and fight with her own demons. So it was easier to focus on someone else than on her own shortcomings.

Vivian hated when Mrs. Woodard would give her that look as if to say, *"You know better than to be out of the church for as long as you have.*

Your mother and father would turn over twice in their graves if they knew you quit the church"

Vivian recalled how her parents would spend their last ten dollars some weeks to make sure Vivian received piano lessons. Vivian was a gifted musical child. She knew how to play most of the church hymns on the organ and piano by the time she was 11 years old. She could read music and she could play by ear. As a result, by the time she was 14 years old, she was leading the entire adult choir and the youth choir at her home church Antioch Church in Southlake's neighboring town of McKinney. She had a beautiful contralto voice and she could sing with vibrato and belt out acrobatic musical scats and runs with ease, which would move the small congregation of Antioch to tears on Sunday mornings. Vivian loved getting her paycheck for her services. By the time she was 16 years old, she was making one hundred dollars a week. Her pastor wanted to make sure that she remained at Antioch for a long time. And she stayed at Antioch as the head musician for over 20 years until she fell out with the new pastor over her church salary. He cut her pay by 30% without a deacon vote and notified her when he gave her the weekly check. She was hurt and humiliated that a new pastor could come into Antioch and dismiss her loyalty and faithfulness like a man trying to swat a pesky fly. Not one of the deacons had stood up on her behalf and most of them had known of her dedication to Antioch. The following Sunday, she came to play the organ, but couldn't get out of her car and she cried in the parking lot as the members passed her up on their way to the church and no one, not a sister, a deacon or even the new pastor came to see if she was okay. An hour later, she drove off and she has never stepped foot in another church in over ten years.

Mrs. Woodard saw the discomfort in Vivian's face and she prayed that God would heal her pain and deliver her from resenting the church.

"Yeah, Vivian I guess everywhere we go there will be rules," said Mrs. Woodard trying to calm the atmosphere. She saw a small tear fall from Vivian's eye, as Vivian quickly began to talk about her latest trip to the Louisiana Casinos and the $2,000 she won on the slot machines.

Chapter 8

The Balancing Act

It was Wednesday night and Lance would be home late tomorrow night. I did not feel like going to bible study tonight. I always feel like the church members think I am spying on them if I attend worship or bible study without Lance. The kids seemed to enjoy the reprieve to stay home from church. I am getting worried about Lance Jr. He is beginning to show signs of resentment toward the church. Today, he came to me and showed me where he received a D+ on his English paper. He said if we didn't have to go to church the night before his paper was due he would have been able to check his paper and possibly made an A on it.

I looked at him coolly and said, "Sweetie, you knew we were going to church last Wednesday night. We go to church every Wednesday night. Why didn't you properly plan to do your English paper?"

"Mom, I was just too busy and church takes up too much of my time. I don't practice baseball as much as we go to church. Why do I have to go to church four times a week?"

Lance insisted that Junior be a part of the junior deacons, usher ministry, and the musical staff, because he was a gifted drummer.

So yes, Junior did spend a lot of time at the church. He spent more time at the church than I did.

"And besides, Mom, they don't like us anyway," Junior said.

"What makes you say that?"

"I overheard Sister Finley and Sister Pepperdine talking about the appreciation services and how they don't think that is necessary to have an appreciation service. They said that Daddy makes enough money during the week and he didn't deserve any more money with all the confusion he has caused around New Light. Then they said that they were sick of you parading around in you hats like you were Queen Elizabeth."

"Junior, stop it! And don't repeat such slandering gossip. It is not worth repeating to anyone. Not even to me."

"Well, I think you should know how these folks feel about us. All that fake and phony love they show us. It's not for real. Even I can see that, Mama," said Junior.

"Come here," I said as I wrapped my child in my arms. I hugged him real tight and looked him squarely in the eye.

"We are here in Southlake, Texas at the New Light Church to serve. We are servants of the most High God. Sometimes in our service, everyone is not going to be pleased with everything we do and that's okay. We serve to bring someone to Christ and to give glory to God. I promise you, Junior, your service will not be in vain. But you have got to learn to not let people's opinions of you or your service distract you from serving Jesus. Our goal is to please Christ.

Satan wants to cut off your service so that you will not be a key player in kingdom building. I'm sorry you had to over hear those two women talking about our family. Just learn to pray for them. Learn to see their needs and look beyond their faults."

My 14-year-old son, my firstborn, my quiet one, silently cried in my arms. "Mom, I love Jesus. I do. But I hate to have to hear some of the things the Christians say about you and Dad," he said.

"Part of being a Christian is being able to withstand criticism, good and bad. Junior, never let someone else's opinion of you or what others say about you, stop you from serving Jesus. It is a trick of the enemy. Look beyond the person and look at the purpose of the words, and the spirit behind them. We are in a spiritual battle between good and evil."

I knew then that it was time to introduce my son to Frank Peretti's debut novel, *"In This Present Darkness,"* a Christian fiction story that details the spiritual nature of principalities and the consistent battles between good and evil. It is a great read to learn about the forces of good and evil as it relates to the bible.

"I want you to study Ephesians Chapter six and I want you to focus on the 12th verse of chapter 6 which says, *For we wrestle not against flesh and blood, but against principalities, against powers, against the rulers of the darkness of this world, against spiritual wickedness in high places,"* I said.

"Junior, I also want you to balance and prioritize your time. A responsible young adult knows how to set priorities and daily goals to reach their purpose in life. Now, I watch you spend at least two hours some days playing video games and another hour and half watching television. That's time where you could be studying your schoolwork especially if you know it is going to be a busy church week. If you promise me that you will work on prioritizing, I will talk to your dad about all the extra time you spend at church and we will get his opinion on what we can do to help you prioritize."

"Thanks, Mom. I just want to be able to do my very best in school. Most of my friends at school don't even attend church, so they don't know how busy our schedules can be with the church. Most of the time, I feel that I am rushed to complete my work, while my friends have all weekend to chill, relax and spend time researching for our school projects," responded Junior.

"Okay. We will both talk to your father about this," I said.

Here was my oldest child, my beautiful baby boy, learning at the tender age of 14 to prioritize and make God number one in his life. I learned early the importance of balance. I didn't want Junior to grow up resenting the church and eventually running away from it. This was my fear concerning all of my children. Lance and I worked hard to ensure that our kids are involved in sports and other community events as well as the church. We both feel that it is important to expose our kids to other positive things in the community. Southlake, fortunately, is a great place to raise a family. The average income in Southlake is over $65,000 a year. There are three golf courses, two country clubs, twelve churches, and one upper scale Mall of Southlake. It boasted a six-year exemplary rating of its school district and a winning sports tradition. Junior loved Southlake ISD when he first enrolled in the eighth grade. He enjoyed being on the football and basketball teams. He was recently voted class president for his upcoming freshman year at Southlake High. We are all hoping that he goes to the University of Texas at

Austin and follow in our footsteps as a fellow Longhorn. This was my baby, my beautiful baby boy. Children grow up so fast. One day you are teaching them how to walk and then the next day you are teaching them how to iron their clothes.

I've learned to appreciate the time I have with my children. There was a time I took my babies for granted. In the early years of his pastorate, Lance and I were so busy in the church, trying to see to the needs of the people of the church that we soon realized that the television and our baby-sitters were raising our children. We rarely sat at the table to eat together as a family except on Sundays after church.

I remember when Junior was about eight years old and he went to a friend's house for the weekend. Upon his return home, I asked him if he had a good time and he said, 'Yeah, it was alright, except for the fact that Jonathan's parents talk too much. They made us eat at the table for every meal and we couldn't even watch the television while we ate. So we were forced to talk to them."

Needless to say I was ashamed that my son thought that eating in front of the television was in his eyes, family time. Soon afterward, I made it a goal to cut out TV at least once a week and have dinner and breakfast together as a family at least four times a week. Lance and I were so consumed with the church and the things of the church that we didn't realize that our home life was out of order and our children were being taught that this was normal.

I have learned to pay attention to all of our children's needs. My Big-mama Thompson would always tell me, "Jackie, you need to learn to build up your house. Do not build your house on sand, but build your house on a solid rock and that rock is Jesus. Chile, you do need to teach your children about Jesus but you also need to show them how to live and make a living for themselves. You have no business being at that church five nights a week with small chillin'. You need to make sure that you are giving them chillin' a healthy balance in their lives. Mary and Joseph did it for their children and you need to do it for your chillin'. Jesus, himself was a carpenter. He had a trade. His Mama and Daddy knew from his birth that He was divine, but they still made sure that he knew how to make a living for himself. Now, Jesus didn't have to work if he didn't want to because he was God in the flesh but yet he did. The bible says, a man that won't work, won't eat. The one thing that I hate to see is lazy, resentful preacher chillin'."

Bigmama T would tell me these things to make sure I invested in my children so that they wouldn't turn into those hellion type preacher kids that are often the gossip of conversations. Bigmama T was so concerned that her beloved great-grandchildren would turn into a resentful wild group of children. That reminded me I needed to call her this week. She is turning 84 next month and she did tell me that she had a chauffeur, a deacon from her church, who was going to drive her and my mama up for Lance's 1st appreciation service at New Light. If I knew my Bigmama she was probably trying to fix my mama up with that deacon chauffeur. My mama said that if she couldn't rise up my deceased father, John Montgomery from the dead, then no other man would suffice for her. She'd rather live her life as a widow. Bigmama T knew that time would heal my mama's lonely heart, but it hasn't stopped her from trying to marry off my mama ever since my daddy's death. Bigmama T was always trying to fix my mama up with one man or another from the Richmond churches or the community. At 60 years old, my mama is a beautiful woman. She is a perfect size ten and stands at 5'6 inches tall. She has natural golden brown hair with a gray streak down the side like the black actress, Della Reese. Men, young and old still exhale when my mama, Eva Montgomery, walks into a room. My mother still lives in her dream home with my younger sister and her two kids. Now, mama's world revolves around them.

I had informed Bigmama T and my mama about how much nicer the people were at this church than Lance's previous pastorates. I also told them how great our children were adjusting to the city of Southlake and how much they liked it. We had moved over three different times in the last 12 years and my children were grateful for any stability. I told them how Lance had fixed up the parsonage and how we were planning to own our first home together in the next five years. I told them that over 40% of our church members had some type of college degree, professional training or trade school certificate and forty-five percent of our church members were consistent tithers. I then told her how we had started with only about 150 active members and now we have grown in less than a year to more than 300 active members. I have learned that good news traveled faster than bad news sometimes so I have learned to be optimistic particularly with my family. They had a tendency to blame Lance whenever I was unhappy or when I complained. Bigmama T was looking forward to coming to Southlake and I sure was looking forward to her visit. I loved to hear her pray those sing-song prayers and I knew that New Light would love my Bigmama and my mama too.

I was determined *not* to share with them my concerns about the controlling Sister Finley or the woman in the red suit that recently joined that Sister Peterson had warned me about. For the last two Sundays, that sister in the red suit always had something to say to Lance after service. I decided that it was better just to pray about these things or write them in my journal than to share my deep concerns with anyone, not even my closest relatives. Sometimes when we speak those things to someone else, Satan and his vices will hear it and use it against us in their spiritual warfare, so it's better to keep it in our spirit and talk to the Lord about it. One thing I know is that Satan cannot read our minds, but he has been playing this game long enough to be able to predict or try to set up what can or could occur to stop the saints of God from enjoying our victory.

Chapter 9

Another Lonely Night

Dear Jesus,

Our appreciation services are now two weeks away. Lord, give me patience to deal with all the issues that can arise out of an appreciation day for the pastoral family. Lance will be in tonight from his revival. Give him safe travel, Jesus. I pray for Lance Jr. that you will help him to find proper balance in his life. Lord, be with us as we prepare to talk to his Daddy about his time for school. Watch over my two babies, Connie, who adores praising you, Jesus. Lord, you have given her such a spirit of praise and worship and Jaylyn who is blooming into puberty. I pray tonight for my mother, my sisters and my Bigmama T, keep them in your loving arms. I also pray for the woman in the red suit. I pray that she will find the counsel she needs and that her motives are pure. Give me peace about her Lord. I also pray that Sister Peterson stops sending me notes about the woman in the red suit every Sunday. Though it is kind of unnerving that this woman since the Sunday she joined our church, wears a different variation of a red suit every Sunday. She is clad with a red suit, a matching red hat, red shoes and a red handbag. I must say this woman has style, but I wonder why she loves the color red so much. I have tried to introduce myself to her but she seems to avoid me or walks away when she sees me heading in her direction. I know Lord that people have their issues, but I wouldn't harm

a fly. So as a result of her distance, I have decided that perhaps she wants her privacy and so I will respect that. I pray Jesus that you dispatch your angels to provide protection over my family and over our church family. In your name, in your will, I do pray.
Love,
Jackie S.

Lately, the woman in red is beginning to be a bit unnerving for me. I did find out that her name is Marilyn Steele and she is originally from Miami, Florida. She is 34 years old and recently relocated to Southlake due to a job transfer. She is a software engineer with a Bachelor of Science degree from Florida A&M University and a Master's degree from Brown University. Sister Peterson just happened to be walking by the new member's class one Tuesday night and managed to hear Sister Steele give her introduction to the class.

"My name is Marilyn Steele. I relocated to Southlake to take a job as a lead engineer with Verizon. I am originally from Miami, Florida. I don't have any family in Texas. My closest living relative is in Alexandria, Louisiana. I did not grow up in the church. I was only truly converted when I joined New Light. I saw the advertisement about New Light riding in my car; I saw the billboard about seeking the light of Jesus. I left Miami, where I was in a dark world and I relocated to Texas for some hope and a new direction. I hope I am in the company of new family and friends," she said.

"Amen, my sister. You are home," my husband said. Sister Peterson just raised her eyebrows and shook her head, as she continued to get their meals ready for the meeting fellowship after their class in the kitchen, which was right next to the new member's classroom. And she said she started singing her code word song while she prepared their food. The song Sister Peterson sings when she spots a women in the church who may be after the married men in the church, is an old Negro spiritual that begs the question of "What is Jesus to you?" Sister Peterson said she started singing it right after Sister Steele gave her welcome introduction to the New Member's Class.

> *I don't know what Jesus is to you.*
> *But I hope He is to you what He is to me. He's my all, my all and all.*
> *He's my chief cornerstone.*
> *I don't know what Jesus is to you, but I hope he is to you-*
> *What He is to me.*

My husband makes it mandatory that every new member of New Light comes through an eight-week new membership class. Sister Peterson let me know that Marcus & Juanita Graves are currently enrolled in the class along with about 25 other new members that have joined in the past few months. Sister Peterson routinely makes it her business to volunteer to bring food to the new member class sessions. I think she goes just to be nosy and to spy on some of the women folks who join our church. My husband has learned to just put up with old Sister Peterson and her ways of trying to pry into people's lives. Besides, he loves the way she makes her signature sweet potato pies and peach cobblers that she brings to the class fellowship meetings. However, he can't stand it when she starts singing her signature song while preparing the food.

My husband will be home tonight from his revival. I bought a sexy red silk pajama set with a matching robe and scarf. I even bought him a purple silk pajama set with matching purple house shoes. I have his bubble bath ready with soft music by, Marvin Gaye, his favorite secular artist, playing in the background. The kids are fast asleep. I can't remember if he told me he would be home Thursday or Friday morning. I know my Lance is going to love my French Roll. I looked myself over in the mirror. At 165 lbs and 5'6, I still looked fairly decent for my age. If only I could lose these love handles around my sides. I was blessed with beautiful hair, teeth and nails all inherited from my mother. I keep them manicured and clean. I made sure to attend a full body spa at least three times a year. I know my Lance would be pleased with my look. Its 11:30pm and Lance is still not back from Austin. Suddenly the phone rang.

"Hello," I said.

"Hi, Sweetheart. Look, I think I am going to spend another night in Austin. I am really tired from preaching and I could use the rest. This last sermon took a lot out of me. I am going to leave tomorrow around 10am so I should get home about 1pm or 2pm."

"But Lance what about our morning together? I took off from work tomorrow morning as a surprise just to be here with you."

"Okay, baby, I'll go ahead, get dressed, and check out of this hotel. I'll call you when I'm halfway home," Lance said as I heard him getting out of his bed.

"No honey. I know you are tired," I reluctantly said. "Get some rest and your Goldie will be waiting for you. Of course the kids will be home, but I will still be here."

"Maybe we can go to a nice dinner or something tomorrow night, baby," Lance said.

"Tomorrow is Lance Jr.'s basketball game, did you forget?" I asked

"You are mad with me. I can tell in your voice that you are disappointed with me," Lance said yawning.

"No I am okay. I'll see you tomorrow afternoon, sweetie" I said. "You just get some rest. I'll be fine. I probably need some rest too. I love you."

"I love you, too Goldie. Goodbye," Lance said.

My dear, all of this preparation and he is a no show. I must admit, I have learned to be flexible with Lance's religious vocation and his time. Preaching can be a very draining employment for those who take it seriously. I have seen Lance study at least 10 hours a week for one sermon or even more than 15 hours if he has a week- long revival. After a revival he is usually exhausted and is not very communicative with anyone for at least a day. When he first started preaching, this routine of Lance's not wanting to communicate almost drove our marriage toward a divorce. My Bigmama Thompson would tell me, "Girl, you just need to learn your husband. Find out what makes him tick. Learn his routine. Stop hollering and screaming, but study that man before you make a move to try to help him."

So that is exactly what I did. I studied my man and I still do at times. I learned that if he has a big church association assignment, how he would be like a kid on Christmas day and sometimes his other priorities, like bill payments might routinely be forgotten. So it's typically during these times, that I will just pay a little something extra on our bills just in case Lance forgot to pay for them. This was early in his pastoring days and he had to learn how to balance his family and the church. I was tired of coming home and the gas would be off. A couple of times, I came home from work and our phone and lights would be off too. It wasn't always because we didn't have the money or that the church didn't have the money. It was typically because our church board was either too lazy to keep up with the bills and Lance was so involved with his studying for school and his sermons that he didn't check on them to make sure our parsonage bills were paid.

Oh, Lord, here I go again reminiscing about the bad things because I am disappointed right now. I wish I had more friends to spend time with. Most of my friends are in Austin, Houston and Richmond, Texas. My best friend, Amanda lives in Los Angeles, California. I must admit I am quite lonely here in Southlake. I haven't found one good friend here since we have relocated. The women of New Light are nice to me, but I am hesitant to get close with anyone for fear of betrayal or that others might persecute them because they are my friends. So my husband, my children, my new job and my trusted journal, 'The First Lady: Joy for the Journey' are the persons I spend most of my days with. Here recently, Lance would on average be out of state preaching at least one weekend out of every month and he averaged one revival every month in Texas. Our times alone to-gether were constantly being circumvented by his growing minis-try calendar.

I folded up Lance's new purple pajamas and placed them neatly in his drawer. I went to the heated temperature controlled whirlpool bathtub and let the water drain out. I swept up the red rose petals that I had delicately placed on the floor and I turned off the Marvin Gaye CD that was crooning ever so silently the song, "Distant Lover." I pulled off my sexy nightgown and put a scarf around my hairdo. I washed off my makeup and mechanically brushed my teeth. I then climbed into my familiar cotton pajamas and slipped under the covers until sleep overcame my tears of loneliness.

Chapter 10

My Purpose

Since Lance did not want my secretarial services at the church, we decided four months ago that I would interview to lead the church sponsored part-time temporary agency called, *Victorious Workers*. I interviewed for the supervisor position and I was hired as director of Victorious Workers. I presently work about 25 hours a week in a small office next to the Southlake Outlet Mall. I help to train assist persons with preparing for interviews and I have just contracted out two workers to a local department store in the outlet mall. My specialty is grant writing. I wrote a grant through our 501c3 organization that Lance organized within the first four months of his pastorate at New Light and this grant was enough to pay for my salary, a part time assistant and lease office space. The church members were very impressed with their new pastor's leadership ability, but I don't think they liked the fact that the pastor's wife would be employed through their newly formed organization.

I thought Sister Finley would have a heart attack, when Lance announced who would lead the first business our 501c3 would support.

"Good morning, brothers and sisters," Lance said during the 11:00 am morning worship pastoral emphasis period.

"The Deacon board and I are happy to announce that my wife, Sister Jacqueline Stevens, will lead our new venture called Victorious Workers, a temporary agency, established to help train and equip our people for quality, successful employment. Sister Stevens is more than able to get this organization off the ground. She has a Bachelor's Degree in Journalism and Marketing from the University of Texas at Austin and a MBA from the University of Phoenix. She also has a certificate in interior design. And most of all, she loves Jesus and she loves this church and community."

I immediately saw Sister Finley throw Deacon Finley a dirty look that said, "How could you not tell me this information!!" Deacon Finley darted his eyes away from her and said, "Amen, Pastor Stevens."

After church, many of the members came up to me and congratulated me for the new position of Director of Victorious Workers. Of course, Sister Finley just lowered her pink wide-brimmed hat and walked smooth past me without even a customary good-bye. I knew that Deacon Finley would soon have to explain why he voted to elect me as Director of Victorious Workers. Sis Finley had wanted her 22- year-old niece, Kayla Barnes to head this business venture. Kayla was a college senior majoring in education at Southern Methodist University in Dallas and she was presently trying to find employment upon her graduation in May. Sister Finley felt that this job would have been perfect for Kayla and it would keep Kayla active in the church. Rumors were circulating that Kayla had been visiting the newly formed Abundant Joy Fellowship Church in Southlake and Sister Finley was not having any of her family members leave her beloved New Light that was established by her kinfolk. She felt that her family had a duty to stay at New Light and to help it prosper despite having a new pastor with a new vision for the church.

Sister Finley, dressed in a lavender suit with matching J. Renee shoes and hat, calmly walked up to me about two weeks after my husband's announcement of the Victorious Workers leadership and said, "Sister First Lady, I am looking forward to seeing what *you* will do for Victorious Workers. There are not too many times around New Light that our men allow a woman to lead such an unprecedented new ministry. I hope that you will do a great job as the director."

"Yes maam. I am quite honored that our leadership has so much faith in me. With God's help, I pray I will do okay," I replied.

"You know, my Kayla, my deceased sister's child, will be graduating in May and she will be looking for a job. Do you need an assistant to work with you at Victorious Workers?" asked Sister Finley.

"Right now, we are not in a position to hire any additional staff. I recently hired Julie Jones to serve as my assistant," I said.

"You did what!! You hired Julie Jones? She just joined our church two months ago! And she has three babies by three different men and she never married any one of them. That woman, does not come to any of our teaching ministries at New Light. Why would you hire a woman like that to represent my, I mean our church? But you couldn't hire my Kayla, huh?" Sister Finley fired back.

"After much prayer and the completion of the interview process, I felt led to choose Sister Jones as my assistant. Sister Jones attends school at night and that is why you have not seen her at the nightly ministries. But she is enrolled in our church Sunday school," I coolly and carefully responded.

"Do the deacons know about your decision or did you even ask them their opinion?" Sister Finley inquired.

"As Director of Victorious Workers, that decision was left solely up to me," I said.

Sister Finley, calmly walked up to me and whispered in my ear, so that no one else in the sanctuary could hear and she proudly said, "Well, that is the problem, you have too much authority. You wait until I get through with you, my Kayla will soon have your job. You just wait and see!" snickered Sister Finley. She smoothly walked away with a prance in her step while her lavender hat bobbed from side to side.

I turned around and thought, "Woman, you are the picture of evil!" I watched her strut away and I reminded myself to pray a special prayer for her. You know if she had said something like that to me during my first few years of being a pastor's wife I would have either hit her or cried like a baby. But over the years, my skin had become tough and I learned to laugh at ignorance in the church and Sister Finley was definitely ignorant. She was more concerned about power and control then she was about seeing people saved toward Jesus Christ. Since that Sunday, I have learned to kill Sister Finley with kindness. So I was not surprised when Junior told me he overheard Sister Finley talking about us. She is slowly losing her grip on New Light and she is crying like a big fat baby over it. She has seemed to age ten years over the last few months because the lines in her face are beginning to show. The way she has tried to yield power over this church, you would think that her husband was the Chairman of the Deacon Board. Deacon Finley is a deacon and a trustee but has always refused to be Chairman, probably because he knows his power hungry wife would go stone crazy if she had the title of "The Chairman's Wife."

New Light's current chairman is Deacon Theodore Jenkins, his wife passed away five years ago. He is 63 years old and a visiting philosophy professor at Paul Quinn College and a retired tenured professor from Southern Methodist University. He has been a member of New Light for over 40 years and was known as a friend to the preacher man. I love Deacon Jenkins because he is always trying to encourage Lance and me to reach our full potential in the Lord. If he disagreed with anything, he always met with Lance, one on one, and was very professional and Christian at every business and deacon meeting. Lance said that Deacon Jenkins is the kind of deacon that every pastor prays for. He was respectful, intelligent, and slow to anger, loved the Word of God, loved God's people and most of all, was saved and lived a godly life. When we first moved to Southlake, Deacon Jenkins would call us at least twice a week just to see if we needed anything. We were so amazed by his attentiveness and respect for the man of God. When Lance would be out of town preaching for a revival or mission trip, Deacon Jenkins would always drop by the parsonage to give me a couple of dollars to take the kids out to eat so I wouldn't have to cook. Our kids affectionately call him Uncle Jenkins. Deacon Jenkins did not have any children of his own, so he likes to come to Junior's basketball games to give him encouragement. That reminds me I need to call him and remind him about Junior's game tonight. Let me call him right now. I called Deacon Jenkins's number, which was now imprinted in my memory from calling so many times over this past year. He answered after the third ring.

"Hello, Deacon Jenkins, I was calling to remind you about Junior's game tonight at 7pm," I said.

"Sister First Lady, I already have my ticket to the game. I'll see you at courtside tonight. Did the good reverend make it in last night?" he asked.

"No, he will be in later on this afternoon. He is planning to attend Junior's game tonight."

"The reverend hasn't come to but four of Junior's games all season and now his season is almost over. We have got to get that man to slow down and spend some time with his boy. A boy needs his father," said Deacon Jenkins.

"Pray for him, Deacon. He has been really pushing himself with all of these revivals and he is often quite drained and tired," I said.

"I know, but I hate for Junior to scan the stands looking for his daddy and all he sees is this old man with peppered gray hair and a graying beard," he said.

"You know, Junior loves when you come to his games. You know how he adores you, deacon."

"I know, but that boy will be in high school next year and I think he has a real shot to go to a Division I school for college and the boy is going to need his daddy to help him with that decision," he said.

I was starting to feel uncomfortable as Deacon Jenkins made me seem like a single woman. My husband *was* out in the field bringing souls to Christ. He was encouraging the saints and providing inspiration. He was kingdom building. But somewhere in my spirit I longed for my husband's presence to be with my son at every game and every outing. Too many times, I was the only one putting together the birthday parties, going to the school plays and the sport activities. I guess I had grown accustomed to supporting my children in ways that their father couldn't because his employment kept him away. I understood that this life was a sacrifice of service. However, when he returned home he was always keenly interested in anything he had missed that his children were involved in.

"Sister First Lady. Are you okay? I didn't offend you, did I?" asked Deacon Jenkins.

"Oh, deacon, I am fine," I said as I silently wiped a tear away. I am glad he couldn't see my tear drop over the phone.

"I'll see you at the game tonight, 7:00 pm straight up. And wear your red, white and blue for school spirit. The high school coaches from Southlake High will be in attendance tonight so it is a big game for Junior," I quickly said.

"Okay, sister, I will see you tonight."

Chapter 11

The Schemers

Mr. Jenkins put the phone on its cradle and looked out of his kitchen window. Sister Jacqueline Stevens was too fine of a lady to leave at home alone too often. Deacon Jenkins loved for her to strut in her hats on Sunday Mornings in grand style. She was always meticulously dressed even if sometimes her eyes had a hint of loneliness in them. Yet and still, when she first arrived at the church, First Lady Stevens's hats were the talk of the New Light Church. Her hats made Sister Finley's hats look like snake feathers. He knew that Sister Finley didn't respect Sister Stevens because she secretly felt that Sister Stevens was trying to always upstage her with her fashion sense. Sister Stevens had to have over one hundred hats, because he could not remember her wearing the same hat twice.

"I'm so sick of these old women in church trying to compete with these younger women in the church," said Deacon Jenkins out loud to himself. *Where are all the women found in the book of Titus, who are supposed to be supportive and teaching these young women? Thought Deacon Jenkins.*

"Boy, who were you talking to?" asked Betty Jean Pepperdine, Deacon Jenkins' older sister who had moved in with him after his beloved wife passed away. She came into the kitchen and began to prepare their afternoon meal.

"I was just thinking about, how we need more Titus Women in our church to train up our young women in the church," said Deacon Jenkins.

"What are you trying to say, Jenkins, that we don't have any Titus women at New Light? We have plenty Titus women at the church. Sister Finley and I are classic examples of Titus women, talked about in the Holy Bible, Titus chapter two. We can't help it if those little young thangs out there won't listen to us. I know I have tried to counsel them young ladies at our church about 'shacking and smacking' but do they listen? No! They go right ahead and let them young men live with them without the sanctity of marriage. They just let the man have his milk and drink it too. So he doesn't have to buy the cow because the milk has been given to him freely on a daily basis," explained Sister Pepperdine.

Sixty-eight year old, Sister Betty Jean Pepperdine was a life long member New Light. She was a retired schoolteacher of the Southlake Independent School District and served on the Usher Ministry and Senior Mission group. She was affectionately known as, Mama Pepperdine by the children of New Light because she did not have children of her own and over the years she was a strong supporter of the New Light Youth Department and their community events. It was not odd to see Mama Pepperdine at a Southlake football or basketball game cheering one of New Light's kids on. She made it her business to find out their games and events so she could cheer them on and encourage them. She had served as one of Youth matrons for over 40 years.

She and Sister Sarah Finley were high school classmates and best friends. They had been there for each other for their weddings, the births of Sister Finley's children and Sister Pepperdine's husband's funeral ten years ago. She and her brother, Deacon Jenkins, decided to move in together about a year ago to cut out extra expenses during their retirement years, since they were both now widowed. Sister Pepperdine and Deacon Jenkins were still getting used to the idea of living under the same roof again.

Deacon Jenkins remembered how bossy his sister was when they were growing up together. She was the oldest of the five Jenkins children and daily let her siblings know who was left in charge over them during their childhood days.

"All I am saying Betty Jean, is that over 75% of the traditional black church is now filled with women. And so we will need more Titus women to teach the women of our church about dress inside the church walls, how to be good wives and good mothers," said Deacon Jenkins.

"Did you see that young woman last Sunday strolling into the church with an orange pantsuit on with no sleeves on her arms? I thought Sarah was going to have a heart attack when she saw that woman coming around the offering plate with that on. Or that other woman who had her skirt hiked up so much in the back, I though old man Johnson was going to be able to see again through his glaucoma laced eyes, he was looking so hard at her," laughed Sister Pepperdine.

"You see, this is what I am talking about. You all will talk about these women but have you tried to get close to them to form a relationship so then you will be able to minister to them? We are getting a lot of people in our church who have never been in the church at any other time in their lives. This is the age of the first unchurched generation in America," explained Deacon Jenkins.

"Please, Jenkins don't go getting on your soapbox this morning. Leave your philosophy for your college class. I know what you are saying, but they don't want to hear some old woman telling them how to dress in the sanctuary. They probably won't listen so why waste our time. We just make sure that we set an example before them and that is why you see Sarah and I always decked out in our Sunday best, with our matching J-Renee shoes and hat. Plus, our hair is always coifed or curled to perfection."

"Do you mean, your wigs, Betty Jean?" laughed Deacon Jenkins.

"Wigs, fake buns, whatever! I bought the hair and so it's mine," snapped Sister Pepperdine. She hated that in the last two years, her hair had thinned so bad she had to resort to wearing wigs to cover up her bald spots. Today, she was sporting a streaked blond, brown chestnut weave that bounced to her shoulders. Sister Pepperdine walked two miles at least three times a week to maintain her size 16 build she possessed since the age of 19. She knew that if she wanted to, she could probably still "catch" her a man but those days were over and her brother's company was all the man that she needed right now. However, she loved to still get the "cat calls" from some of those older men in the church and the Southlake community who had been recharged due to the invention of Viagra.

"All I am saying Jenkins is that these young women of Southlake are not in to us old women and they don't want to hear what we have to say. Besides you can let First Lady Stevens talk to them, she needs something to do, something besides wearing her hats on Sunday.

Let her talk to those young ladies. She is probably not much older than most of them. She rarely comes to Sunday school anymore and she hardly comes to the Mission group but yet she wants to be over Victorious Workers. I still haven't figured that one out. So, I guess if she is not running things she doesn't want to participate in them," said Sister Pepperdine.

"Girl, you need to stop listening to Sarah's crap because now it sounds like, you don't care for Sister Stevens," said Deacon Jenkins.

"I know that Sarah doesn't too much care for the First Lady, but she does make a point about her. She has been here almost a year and she hardly says two words to anyone. She doesn't work with our children in the church, she doesn't even try to help us serve in the kitchen or help clean up. She just sits there and wears her hat like she is a queen or something. And why do *we* have to fix the Pastor's plates and his family a plate after church fellowships? She is young enough to make her own plate and fix her family a plate including her husband," explained Sister Pepperdine with her hands on her hips waiting for a response.

She knew that Jenkins wouldn't say too much. He was always fiercely loyal to any pastor that had graced the pulpit of New Light. But lately he was consistently taking up for Sister Stevens and defending her a little too much. Anytime she said one thing about Sister Stevens or her children, Jenkins was quick to change the subject. Some of the members were beginning to call the house and talk to Jenkins about the First Lady's inactivity. And many were surprised to learn that she was willing to lead Victorious Workers and wondered if such a quiet pastor's wife had the guts to lead a company successfully.

"It's not easy being a pastor's wife, Betty Jean. You just need to pray for her. Her purpose right now may be to nurture her children and tend to their needs," explained Deacon Jenkins.

"If that is the case, then why is she taking the time to lead Victorious Workers?" quizzed Sister Pepperdine.

"Just try to pray for them, Betty. Can you do that?" said Deacon Jenkins as he abruptly stood up from the table.

"I still don't understand, why Sarah's niece, Kayla Barnes didn't get that Director's job for Victorious Workers," said Sister Pepperdine trying to get some answers from her beloved Deacon Brother.

"That is official church business and you don't need to know the reason why she didn't get the job" said Deacon Jenkins.

"Well, I'm a 65 year member of New Light and I pay my tithes every month from my trust fund, pension and my social security check, so if I want my church to tell me why someone was hired over someone else I think I have a right to know. I am sick of you men folk at that church trying to keep everything from us women in the church!" shouted Sister Pepperdine.

"Because for one, Betty, yawl talk too much and you can't hold water! That's why we don't tell the women anything. If you all were prayer warriors, maybe just maybe we would give you the inside scoop. But you women would find a way to gossip even during your public prayers," said Deacon Jenkins.

"All I know is, if it weren't for the women of New Light, you 25 or on a good day 45 men of New Light wouldn't even have a church. So call us what you want, we are still the majority in the church," rebuffed Sister Pepperdine.

"We may be in the minority in the church, but God gave us the authority and some of you, like you and Sister Finley need to learn to be silent in the church. And if Sarah wouldn't talk so much in the church, she wouldn't get misquoted so much. One thing about it, you can't misquote silence," said Deacon Jenkins as he straightened his chair and put it underneath the kitchen table.

"I bought us two tickets to Lance Jr.'s game tonight" He quickly said trying to change the subject.

"I have other plans already for tonight, so I won't be going," replied Sister Pepperdine.

"What do you mean you are not going to his game? Betty you go to all of the other New Light kids' games but you have yet to attend any of Lance Jr. games. You know this is his first year playing for Southlake and you are the kids' favorite youth matron. And you know how those kids brag about how you attended one of their games and screamed the loudest. And this is the second time I have bought you a ticket and you haven't gone to Junior's game. Are you deliberately trying to hurt Junior?" Deacon Jenkins questioned.

"From what I hear, his own preacher daddy hardly attends any of his games, so I know Junior will hardly miss seeing me there tonight," fired Sister Pepperdine. "I told you Jenkins, I have other plans tonight, so just invite someone else to go with you."

"Woman, you and I both know you will be sitting here tonight on that phone gossiping with Sarah about the church," said Deacon

Jenkins. "I'm going over to Thelma's Diner for lunch," he said as he walked out slamming the screen door behind him.

"What about my chicken & dumplings and cabbage I'm slaving over here trying to fix for us?" hollered Sister Pepperdine out of the kitchen window.

"Eat it yourself!" Deacon Jenkins hollered back.

Sister Pepperdine watched Jenkins drive off in his Mercedes Benz SUV and thought to herself.

I don't know what has gotten into Jenkins lately. Every time I said a word about the pastoral family he would get so protective of them. And why should I go to Junior's game. I know he heard Sarah and me talking about his mama and daddy. I saw the boy eavesdropping on us after we had our conversation and since that time I can hardly look the boy in the eye. If I went to his game, he would know that I wasn't being sincere so why even try to pretend I supported him by attending the game when the boy already heard me gossiping about his parents? I just have a funny feeling that he told his mama, First Lady Stevens. For the last two Sundays, Sister Stevens has been syrupy sweet to me and making a point to smile in my face and hug me, which is something she would normally not bother to do. Besides, I do have plans tonight. Sarah and I have plans to go to the church and clean and we hired a contractor to surprise the Pastor for his first year appreci-ation services by buying him a new desk, computer, a color TV and a few other surprises. Sarah thought a soft baby blue was a soothing color for an office that was used to counsel the members. Sarah has an associate degree in Psychology so she is always trying to use her knowledge of colors and its effects in her decorating. I believe she is still upset that that the Pastor and First Lady had the parsonage repainted in another color after Sarah and her hired contractor painted it a soft baby blue and pink. Sarah said that the Pastor's new office color, complete with a new desk and accessories was supposed to be a surprise, but I pray that it is not pay back toward the Pastor and First Lady for being ungrateful for her gift of painting the parsonage when they first moved into the house. Surely, Sarah wouldn't stoop that low and still call herself a Christian. I need to call her and see what time we are going to meet at the church tonight to begin our surprise extreme makeover of the Pastor's office.

Sister Pepperdine dialed Sister Finley's number.

"Hello?" answered Sister Finley.

"Good Morning, Sarah, how are you doing?"

"Girl, the Lord is blessing me this morning. I have the contractor in place and he is painting as we speak and the Pastor's new furniture has arrived by truck this morning. So I let the contractor in the Pastor's office this morning at 9:00am and afterward the movers will put the furniture together and trash his old desk. I think he is really going to be surprised!" said Sister Finley.

"How did you get a key to Pastor's office?" Sister Pepperdine asked.

"My sweet, dear Abraham, left his master key to the church in his pants pocket and when I went to wash his pants, the key miraculously fell on the floor and I miraculously made a copy of it," laughed Sister Finley. "My family sacrificed too much for this church for a living member of our family not to have a copy of our sweet beloved New Light master key. I have a right to this key," declared Sister Finley. "And I don't care what Abraham Finley or that new Pastor of ours has to say about it."

"Won't they know that you have a master key after the makeover of the office?" asked Sister Pepperdine.

"Our Pastor may just assume that my husband opened up the office for me and believe me, my Abraham will be too embarrassed to tell anyone that his wife may have her *own* key to the Pastor's office. I can handle my Abraham."

Did you find anything in our Pastor's office that might be a little secretive?" quizzed Sister Pepperdine.

"I did find a small safe in his office but I could not crack it open. I tell you, our new Pastor is smart. Other than that, the boy is squeaky clean. I did notice that new member, Sister Marilyn Steele's information card on his desk, so I guess they are now communicating. You know I couldn't help but feel that the two of them knew each other when she first joined our church. It was just something in his eyes when he saw her walk forward to join our church that made me think that our Pastor knew this Marilyn Steele woman. My woman's intuition told me that something is familiar between the two of them. I am going to check out a few more things in his office when we return tonight," said Sister Finley.

"Oh, please Sarah, every man in the church is going goo-goo over that woman right now. I am just wondering why she has to always wear different shades of red to church every Sunday. That girl, might be crazy or something," said Sister Pepperdine.

"Maybe she likes the color red, like I like the color pink. Did you know that I own over 30 pink hats?" said Sister Finley.

"Yes, Sarah, I am quite aware of your hat collection. Didn't you like that hat First Lady Stevens wore last Sunday? Now that was a pretty pink hat," said Sister Pepperdine.

"Oh, please those are her grandmother's hats she wears, so therefore it is not her style, but a style she is emulating. She is not an original, like I am," proclaimed Sister Finley.

"Well how do you know where her hats are from? You barely even talk to the First Lady?"

"Well, when I was really talking to her she let me know that her grandmother had willed her a collection of hats. So you see, her style is old and imitated," said Sister Finley.

"But you don't know which hat is willed or purchased, so I think she is still classy," Sister Pepperdine chastised.

"Whatever, Betty Jean. You just want to be in the good graces of the pastoral family because you know your brother would want you to pay respect to them and he wouldn't have it any other way," said Sister Finley.

"Must I remind you that Jenkins is not my husband, nor my daddy? He is my younger brother and I can think what I want to think about anyone," said Sister Pepperdine proudly through her telephone.

She hated when Sarah Finley thought that her brother was controlling her. Just because he was Chairman of the Deacon board and just because he provided a nice two story, four-bedroom home for them to live in and he paid for all of the bills, did not mean that he controlled her.

"Jenkins has his opinions and I have my opinions. And we respect each other's differing opinions, Sarah. So stop trying to insinuate that I don't have my own mind or I am being influenced by Jenkins," Sister Pepperdine said.

"Okay, Betty Jean, don't get all worked up. Now, I need you to meet me at the church at 5:30pm. I talked to the First Lady earlier today who told me that Pastor won't be in until this afternoon and they are going to Lance Jr's game tonight. So that is enough time for us to tidy up his office. I told the church janitor to take the day off and come back on Saturday afternoon to get the church ready for the Appreciation service," said Sister Finley.

"Wow, don't you have a lot of power. When did you start telling church staff to take the day off?" questioned Sister Pepperdine.

"It's easy, when they are too stupid or looking for an excuse not to work. I told him that Pastor told me to tell him to take the day off to spend time with his wife, who is in the hospital battling an episode with her lupus condition," said Sister Finley.

"Girl, you are so bad. God is going to get you for lying on the preacher," said Sister Pepperdine.

"Well it's really not a lie. I overheard Pastor talking to Abraham about letting our church janitor off from work to spend time with his sick wife and so I thought it was perfect timing. I told him to take off Friday, so that we would have time to do our little extreme makeover surprise for the pastor. And while we are remodeling his office, make sure to remind me to take down the First Lady's picture and her personal biography hanging up in his office. I don't understand why she must have her picture and bio up next to the pastor in his office. It's not like we are giving her a salary too. And I told our church secretary to take off the programs the word 'family' for the appreciation service. This celebration is for the Pastor, not his family or God forbid, Pastor and Wife Appreciation Service. Does the wife get up every Sunday and preach to us? Is she ultimately held responsible for our souls? No, she is not, and therefore, we should not appreciate her or her children," said Sister Finley, in her customary sarcastic tone.

"I guess you forgot that we are giving the First Lady a salary now. Remember, she is Director of Victorious Workers," said Sister Pepperdine.

"Oh yes, indeed, how that happened I don't know. I must be losing my grip because that should not have occurred. That reminds me, I need to give Kayla a call to see how she is doing in her job search. That girl, cried like a baby when she found out that she didn't get the job as Director of Victorious Workers. I bought her a $200 black pants suit and J-Renee 3 ½ inch shoes for her interview to impress that interview panel and she still didn't get it. Did you find out from Jenkins why they didn't hire Kayla?" asked Sister Finley.

"Please, Jenkins is not saying a word to me about that matter. And furthermore, I believe the First Lady, does sacrifice being married to the Pastor. She has to be careful with her words, and be discreet while her life is altered by the members' needs as well," noted Sister Pepperdine.

"Does she dress like she is sacrificing for anyone or anything? Is she teaching in the church or even singing in the choir when we all know she can sing? Isn't she and Pastor both dressed to kill every Sunday at church?"

"Well, I guess so, Sarah, but you would talk about them, if they weren't dressed to kill," trailed Sister Pepperdine.

"Please, Betty Jean. They have got it made. They are living in a parsonage, all bills paid. We give them a housing allowance and he was recently approved for a $50 monthly car allowance. Our pastor's aide has agreed to pay for his seminary tuition to obtain his accredited doctorate from Dallas Seminary. Sister Stevens is working for the church outreach business and receiving a nice salary at twelve dollars an hour. They are both riding in nice cars, even if both cars are over eight years old. They are still rolling. But you wait and see, I bet you the next thing he requests will be a new car. I don't see why they can't go out and buy a new car with their own money. They don't have to be dependent on the church for everything," said Sister Finley matter of factly.

"Is that *all* the church is paying Sister Stevens is twelve dollars an hour! Are you serious? Why, that lady has two degrees she could probably earn over $100,000 a year in the secular world!" said Sister Pepperdine.

"She can go ahead and work for a secular company and find another church for all I care. My Kayla should have had that job anyway and if Sister Stevens wasn't the Pastor's wife, that job would have been Kayla's," said Sister Finley. "Meet me at the church around 5:30 and we will talk then."

"Okay, Sarah, talk to you later," said Sister Pepperdine as she gently laid the phone down on the phone rest.

92

"Lord, Jesus, I pray that I am not guilty by association for this," Sister Pepperdine said out loud to herself. She knew that Sister Finley had a good heart, but lately her desire for control and power were taking fast control over her good intentions. Sister Pepperdine returned to the kitchen to finish preparing her lunch that she would now have to eat alone.

Chapter 12

A Beautiful Southern Lunch

It was a beautiful Friday afternoon in Southlake. The birds were chirping, squirrels were playing hide and seek along the curbed streets and there was a clean northeastern Texas breeze flowing through the city. There was not a cloud in the sky and the Texas beauty of the day, seemed to put a smile on every strangers face that entered Southlake. It was on these days of living in Southlake that I was glad we relocated here. I was on my way to eat at Thelma's Diner, since Lance wouldn't be home until mid afternoon from his revival trip. I wore my beige linen A-line pants with a red silk blouse accented with my Indian ruby red jewelry with matching earrings, necklaces and two rings. It was a gift Lance brought back with him from one of his revivals in the state of Florida last year. My hair was in a French Roll and I was strolling in my Red Gucci heeled sandals with my red Gucci belt that completed my look. Today, I felt pretty and professional even if I was now a size 14. I knew it was important to "look" like a Pastor's wife wherever I was out and about in the city of Southlake. My hair, nails and clothes must look polished at all times. The people expected their Pastor and his family to look good at all times. The First Family was a reflection of the church as Sister Sarah Finley constantly reminded me at least once every other month. I had decided to purposefully kill Sister Finley with kindness ever since Junior told me about what he had overheard her and Sister Betty Jean Pepperdine talking about.

I walked into Thelma's Diner to find Deacon Jenkins sitting in a booth by himself reading a paper. I walked over to his booth and sat down.

"Would you like some company, old man?" I asked.

"Sister Stevens, how are you doing? I am blessed to see you in here," replied Deacon Stevens, putting his paper down on the table. "You are looking very pretty today. I love your Indian red accessories. That really looks good on you."

"Why, If I didn't know it, I would think you were flirting with me Deacon," I said with a hint of teasing in my voice and a wink in my eye.

"Girl, I'm old enough to be your daddy, but I have learned to always compliment a good looking woman on a beautiful day like this," said Deacon Jenkins.

The waitress walked over and took our orders.

"I'll have a salad, with red-wine vinaigrette dressing, a small baked potato with the works, and a glass of water with lemon," I said.

"I'll have your chicken fried steak meal and a glass of sweet tea," said Deacon Jenkins. "Thank you."

"I can't believe that you are not home eating one of Sister Pepperdine's famous meals?" I asked. "Is everything all right?"

"Yes, she and I had a little spat that's all. I just needed some air and I was hungry so I came here. How often do you come to Thelma's Diner?" asked Deacon Jenkins.

"I come about once a week and I know Thelma's barbeque ribs are probably the reason I have put on this extra weight."

"You look great, Sister Stevens" Deacon Jenkins said.

The owner of Thelma's Diner, Thelma Henderson was originally from Karnack, Texas and her immediate family was known for their secret family barbeque sauce and their ability to make a great Texas Sausage and delicious ribs. Her macaroni and cheese and baked beans could make a grown man slap himself. She opened up her own restaurant in Southlake about ten years ago and the community of Southlake, blue collar and professional folks alike made her an instant hit in the county. Today it was filled with people on their lunch break and tourists who loved to take pictures of her wall of fame which contained pictures of famous Texans, politicians and entertainers that have dined at her restaurant. Thelma Henderson was a member of New Light and always gave the pastoral family a 50% discount whenever they came to dine at her restaurant. She and Vivian Daniels, owner of Heavenly Hands were second cousins, the granddaughters of two sisters, and had always supported each other in their business. So today, Vivian was eating Thelma's signature Barbeque Ribs, potato salad and baked beans with a cool margarita.

Vivian was seated on the other side of Thelma's and thought it strange when she spotted Sister Stevens with her husband's chairman of the deacon board, Deacon Jenkins eating at the same booth and just chuckling away. Deacon Jenkins might be 63 years old, but in Vivian's eyes he was a King of wealth and intelligence. He was 64 inches tall, with pepper gray hair and a kingly pepper gray beard, light hazel eyes, brown majestic skin, a nicely built piece of man who owned a slamming Mercedes Benz SUV and lived in the "right" community of Southlake in his 4,000 square foot home. Deacon Jenkins just "oozed" money and he was a college professor. He possessed brains, beauty, money and power; a perfect combination and just what Vivian needed and wanted right now. Vivian had to snap out of her dream zone as she wondered what she could do with a man like Deacon Jenkins. Viagra could solve any other problems they might have. Why was he over there just smiling at First Lady Stevens like that? Vivian pondered

Vivian loved a good piece of church gossip to share with her customers. *I may need to see just what is going on over there. Vivian thought.* She coolly walked toward their booth and straightened out her pink & green tunic sundress with her 2-inch heeled pink Star Jones Fioni strap sandals.

"Wow, aren't you two the picture of happiness over here," said Vivian as she walked up to their booth.

"Oh, hi Ms. Vivian. Yes the good deacon and I both happen to be here at the same time and we said why eat alone, when we can eat together" said Sister Stevens with a smile and glow on her face. "This is Deacon Jenkins, our Chairman of Deacons at New Light. Do you two already know one another? I know I am still new to Southlake," I said.

"Hello Ms. Vivian, you are looking mighty nice today. Pink & green are your colors, young lady. And of course we know each other. I've known Vivian since she was a little girl, playing that organ and making it talk, since she was twelve years old. Why, she was our county's first child musical prodigy," said Deacon Jenkins.

"You are so kind Jenkins," said Vivian, secretly wishing that he'd consider now that she was a full grown woman in her late forty's with many needs and wants. And right now, she wanted him and all of his money.

"Mrs. Stevens, why your hair is still gorgeous and you look absolutely fabulous! I love your red accessories. Girl that is your color," said Vivian.

"Why, if it wasn't for Heavenly Hands" said Sister Stevens raising her hands in the air like she was giving a praise shout, "I don't know where I would be," laughed Sister Stevens.

"Thank you, sister. Well, I just wanted to stop by and say hello, its time for me to prepare for my next appointment at the salon. I will see you next week First Lady," said Vivian to Sister Stevens and kissed her on the check.

Then she turned to face Deacon Jenkins, "And as for you, Jenkins, I hope to be seeing you in the near, not so far future," Vivian said with a wink of her eye. "Good day to both of you," Vivian said as she walked off with a little twist in her step just in case the good Deacon was still watching her walk off. When she arrived at the door of Thelma's Diner to exit, she peeked back at the booth to find Deacon Jenkins still watching her with a huge grin on his face and with that, Vivian swung her golden micro braids and laughed as she strutted out of the door. *Yes, she thought to herself. One day, Deacon Jenkins you will be mine, all mine. Maybe it is time to visit New Light Church after all.*

Chapter 13

Anonymous Letters

I came home after having lunch with Deacon Jenkins and walked into my bedroom to retrieve my journal that I placed in one of my secret places of my home. I wrote:

Dear First Lady,

Today, I just shared a great afternoon with Deacon Jenkins at Thelma's Diner. He is really a smart man and I think my hairstylist, Vivian has a slight crush on him. They would make a cute attractive couple. Mr. Jenkins told me that he wasn't much for dating right now because he was still grieving over his late wife, even though more than five years had passed since her death. Perhaps that is something I will pray over for him that he find some female Christian companionship. Tonight is Junior's game and I hope Lance is going to arrive home in time to come to his game. I learned so much about the history of Southlake and New Light from Deacon Jenkins. That man is a walking encyclopedia. He also shared with me about his 40-year marriage to his deceased wife and their travels. They were not able to have any children due to his infertility. It was something that had haunted him most of his adult life that he wouldn't have a son to carry on his name. I asked him why he didn't adopt any children and he said that he and his beloved wife, Doris were so busy giving and tending to the children of New Light that they were like the children they never had. He also explained to me that his sister Betty Jean Pepperdine was not able to conceive any children as well. This was the bond that they shared together, so they lived to help other people raise their kids and had a special relationship, both he and his sister Betty Jean with the children of New Light. I didn't want to bust his bubble and tell him that Betty Jean was overheard by my son talking about our family. I have too much respect for Deacon Jenkins to pass on something negative to him about his sister. Some things are better off not being said at all. I know Sister Pepperdine is loyal to Sister Finley since they grew up together. Sometimes, I long for friendship in my life outside of my family. I am praying for a friend in Southlake who loves me for me and not because I am Pastor Lance M. Stevens Sr.'s wife. So far, I haven't found that kind of companion here.

The minister's wives in the Southlake metropolis area seem so stand offish and are not too friendly. Some of them just talk too much for my taste and I am generally afraid to trust them with anything. For example, just last month, one of the Pastor's wives in McKinney actually got up in the congregation during a banquet held in honor of First Lady McDonald and shared how she and Sister McDonald, a bishop's wife, talked on the phone about their husband's infidelities. Yeah, First lady she really said that! She then said, "My husband may love the Lord, but he also loves the skirts and the butts isn't that right, Sister McDonald." Poor Sister McDonald ran out of the banquet hall crying. Now just imagine, if I had shared some intimate things with her and she told an entire church family. So I have determined to be discreet and try not to bring shame to my husband's ministry and so as a result it can be a lonely life. I am not really active with anything yet at the church. It is by choice, but Lance is really not encouraging my involvement in anything in the church except Victorious Workers, which is outside of the church in another location. At his other churches, I sang in the choir, worked with the youth, mission groups, and played an active part in the Pastor's aide. But it was during the times of my great involvement that I faced my greatest dilemmas with his members. They used me for their own personal agendas and tried to pick and set me up to achieve their own goals. It was at times very confusing and caused me to not trust anyone within the church. It was also a source of great bitterness for me. Now, at New Light, Lance was encouraging me to take it slow and take my time to discover my purpose. Lance thought I needed time to allow the members to get used to me first. I enjoyed singing and sometimes I missed singing in the choir and leading songs. I love giving praise to God. Last week, our new musician, Brother Marcus Graves invited me to participate in the new Praise and Worship Team he was starting. I told him that I would have to speak with my husband about it first. I hadn't bothered to ask Lance, fearing that he would tell me, "No, not now, it's too soon." I guess I will ask him sooner or later. Perhaps I will wait until after the one-year Pastor's Appreciation service this week. I noticed the program just says "Pastor Appreciation Day" and no one has bothered to say anything about his family. I guess I don't mind. Every church does it differently. Typically at the other churches my husband pastored, they would always include the children and me with a poem or something as a token of respect. And the programs usually included a picture of the pastor's family. I know it was probably Sister Finley's idea to exclude the Pastor's Family from the appreciation service programs. The church's new administrative assistant is her distant cousin and I am sure Sister Finley had her to change the programs to delete the Pastor's family. I know that Sister Finley does not care too much for me, but she tries to be respectful. I can tell that it is killing her to even speak to me on Sunday mornings. Every Sunday, she looks me up, and down from head to toe and never says a "You look nice" or anything. She just takes a full view and walks away. I feel like I am being inspected when I am in her presence. I am praying for her because she doesn't realize that she

won't be able to see Jesus if she doesn't learn to love me. I will talk to
you soon, I need to go by the church and get a church membership
record for Victorious Workers. So, First Lady I will talk to you soon
and please keep praying for me…
Love,
Jackie Stevens

I closed my journal and placed it under my bed mattress. One of the secret places I kept it so that I could get to it quickly when I needed it. This journal was my friend and confidante. I wrote my thoughts to the Lord in it and I also talked to the First Lady in it, when I needed some room to separate myself from that title and the pressures that came with it. I found this journal to be very therapeutic. I took a class in psychology while attending the University of Texas and I remember learning that life is full of curves and pitfalls, it does not get any easier, but you have got to find better methods of coping with the pitfalls of life. Destructive habits of coping could lead to death and bitterness. I learned this early in my journey as a minister's wife. I met a Pastor's wife years ago who used alcohol to deal with some of the pressures of being married to a prominent pastor. She was often home alone, while he crises-crossed the country preaching revivals. She had their two children who kept her company, but she often felt like a single woman as she cared and nurtured them. They lived in a prosperous section of Los Angeles, California and lived in a 5,000 square foot home. They both drove luxury cars and yet she was unfulfilled. She loved Jesus but she allowed alcohol to fill her void and before she knew it, she was a raving alcoholic at the age of forty. I will always remember her testimony at a Minister's Wives Conference of drying out at an Alcoholic Anonymous Retreat Center and getting her Christian and family life back on track. Her husband was so busy trying to save other souls, he didn't realize that his own wife had lost fellowship with God and him. I knew that alcohol and other numbing drugs could be a real problem for those who are constantly under the limelight or living in a fishbowl. I make it a point to attend self-help conferences and seminars that cater to clergy wives or Women in leadership just to help me stay encouraged. I remember about learning from one of the Ministry wives Conferences I attended about the infamous anonymous letter that is common among clergy wives.

Lance was pastoring at Little Mt. Zion. We were there four years when my first anonymous letter came in the mail. This letter said that Lance was having an affair with his church secretary at Little Mt. Zion, Sister Sharon Dancey, who was a 32 year old college student who was single with two kids. She had become a great friend to us and often babysat our kids while we traveled during Lance's ministry engagements. "The letter" was typed and it went something like this:

Dear First Lady, or in the words of your husband, I'll call you Goldie, I know you are wondering why I am writing you but you have a right to know that the woman who you think is your friend, Sister Dancey, is not your friend. I have seen your husband pick her up and take her to a local motel in town at least three different times around 2pm. That's right, Goldie, your precious man is cheating on you and right in your face. I just thought you should know that everyone smiling in your face is not who you think they are. So beware and remember to always trust in the Lord. Of course, I cannot leave my name, but my prayers are with you. Handle your business and set that woman straight. Remember, boys will be boys so don't be so hard on the Pastor.

Signed

Anonymous

I remember thinking, *Okay, I am in the sisterhood of the First Ladies Sorority now.* Lance was furious that someone would disrespect our house and his wife by having the audacity to send an anonymous letter. And the usage of the name Goldie is his pet name for me that no one else was allowed to use. He wanted to go to the pulpit on Sunday morning and expose everything and dare anyone to send anything else to our house. I told him that we would not give Satan any time or energy during a service dedicated to worshipping God. Whoever sent that letter wanted attention and wanted to start some friction and I wouldn't dishonor my integrity by getting on their level. I told my husband that I loved him and that I trusted him and a letter could not take that away. Now, if there were problems going on and I had a question about Lance's whereabouts, then *the letter* may have caused me to cringe. But Lance was a good father and a respectful, predictable husband and at 2:00pm every day he was picking up his 3 year old from school. Nevertheless, we shared the letter with his secretary, who was implicated in the letter, Sister Sharon Dancey, who immediately broke into tears and shortly thereafter, one month to be exact, quit her position as secretary and left Little Mt. Zion, because she felt couldn't deal with the drama and mess that came along with being a secretary to a Pastor. Lord knows, that church secretaries may have to deal with as much drama as clergy wives. Lance and I grew together after that episode and we were determined to stay together in spite of vices within and without the church that have tried to separate us. We never discovered the writer of the anonymous letter and neither did we try to find out, but I will tell you I put a prayer on that person that Jesus would take them down like David slew Goliath. I am a firm believer in asking God to fight our battles. And believe me, none of my enemies have ever won against my God. He is my strong deliverer and redeemer. About four months after that I received another anonymous letter which simply said,

Dear Goldie,

I guess you have more class that I thought you did. You need to start taking better care of your man before I do. I know what he needs and what he deserves. I can give him what you are apparently refusing of late, to give him. I saw you at the conference walking around in your big silver hat like a rooster crowing. Let this be a warning, your man is up for grabs and his heart is lonely and his eyes are beginning to wander. Watch your back, sister!

Signed

You Know Who, Anonymous

Soon after this second anonymous letter came, Lance began to check and scan all mail coming to our home. He was furious that someone could be so cruel and keep disrespecting our family. I just laughed it off and wondered what conference this person saw me. I only attend about four or five conferences a year and I couldn't remember for the life of me where I wore a silver hat. Anyhow, I just said a fast and furious prayer that God would bring justice and mercy to the writer of that letter. I know that my God has protected me from many other situations that would seek to destroy and hurt me and so I trust in him completely to guide me and hold me in times of great frustration.

I know that Satan wants to distract believers and the church from our first love, which is bringing souls to Christ. I prayed that I would not get distracted from my focus on God, my family and my community. In my 39 years, I have learned that life is a journey. It is a process. It is a seasonal experience. As King Solomon said in Ecclesiastes 3:1, *"There is a time for everything, a season for every activity under heaven."* I have learned that every experience should be a learning experience and the experience has arrived because God either caused it or has allowed it. God is omnipotent and omnipresent, all at the same time. I have learned to trust him and put my complete faith in him.

I walked over to the music system in our bedroom and turned on Natalie Wilson and SOP's gospel song, "He's Working It Out for You. " I absolutely love that song. I lay on my bed and meditated about my God and all the things that He has done for me. I listened as Natalie Wilson's crooned the song about how God is working every-thing out in our lives. I said a silent prayer that Lance would get home safely from Austin. I thanked God for his blessings in my life. I changed the CD and turned on one of my favorite gospel artists, Chester D. T. Baldwin and listened to his song, "A God of Another Chance" and tears of triumph flowed as I recalled God's grace dur-ing those times where I wanted to give up and walk away from the church. And how God gave me another chance to see Him work in my life and let me see the vision and purpose that He has for my life. I am learning to surrender my all to God on a daily basis so that His will, will be accomplished in my life. It was at this moment that I felt God embrace me as I lay on my bed of meditation and His glory filled my empty space of loneliness. It seemed like I had cried for hours until I opened my eyes from resting to see my husband leaning on one knee, kneeling by my bedside.

"Hello, Goldie," Lance said, kissing me on the cheek.

"Hi sweetheart. You made it home safely. Praise God!" I said through tear stained eyes.

"Are you okay? It looks like you have been crying. Your eyes are red and puffy. " Lance questioned. "Did the light bill get paid, is the gas out, and did the church look after you while I was gone?" he quizzed with a look of worry over his face.

Reaching for my Kleenex that I kept beside my bed, I lightly sat up on the bed and dabbed my eyes. "So many questions and the church treated us fine while you were gone and yes the bills were paid timely this month. I was rejoicing and thanking God for all that he has done for us. You know I remember the parsonage that we lived in when you first pastored a church. Remember how the parsonage was leaking all the time? We had to keep moving Connie's crib around the house so that she wouldn't get wet because we had so many leaks."

"Do I remember?" Lance said rolling his eyes in the back of his head.

"I remember the financial struggles, the small love offerings that we lived by and all the church dramas that God delivered us from and I guess I was overwhelmed by His divine protection and His awesomeness. It has almost been a year now at New Light and God is still blessing us and keeping our family. We don't have everything we want right now but God has delivered on his promise to provide for our needs," I said.

We reminiscenced, while Chester D. T. Baldwin's gospel hit song "God is Good" played in the background. Lance began to sing with the lyrics, *"My God is good all the time. When I woke up early this morning, I thank the Lord for a brand new day!"*

I watched my husband as he changed his travel clothes, removed his suitcase clothes from the suitcase and placed them in the laundry basket to be washed. I settled comfortably on the bed and thanked God for a man who seemed to care so much for ministry work and

I remembered that this was the man I once ran from because I was afraid of being a minister's wife and I didn't want the title or the pressure that came with it. But I looked at Lance and I knew that God had put us together and I prayed that nothing would ever separate us. I knew that if I was to stay connected to God hat I must stay connected to God's Word. I grabbed my bible that I kept on my nightstand and begin to read from the Psalms. I read Psalm 100 out loud:

> *Shout with joy to the LORD, O earth!*
> *Worship the LORD with gladness.*
> *Come before him, singing with joy. Acknowledge that the LORD is God!*
> *He made us, and we are his.*
> *We are his people, the sheep of his pasture. .*
> *Enter his gates with thanksgiving;*
> *go into his courts with praise.*
> *Give thanks to him and bless his name.*
> *For the LORD is good.*
> *His unfailing love continues forever,*
> *and his faithfulness continues to each generation.*

As I read this passage out loud, Lance mocked me like a Southern Baptist proclaimer, "Say it again, Can I get a witness, isn't the Lord good? Yes sah! He is good!"

We looked at each other with adoration as we celebrated this moment of God's word and his wonders! I continued in Lamentations 3:22-25 reading out loud with enthusiasm:

> *The unfailing love of the LORD never ends! By his mercies we have*
> *been kept from complete destruction. Great is his faithfulness; his*

mercies begin afresh each day. I say to myself, "The LORD is my in-
heritance; therefore, I will hope in him!" The LORD is wonderfully
good to those who wait for him and seek him.

All the while Lance sang Baldwin's song, "God is Good" with high energy and he slid across our wooden floors as if he was preaching
with a pretend microphone in his hand. I loved to hear Lance sing.
He was blessed with a beautiful voice. His natural vibrato and his
ability to sing scants and runs could bring any church congregation to their feet. He came to the bed and scooped me in his arms
and kissed me passionately. The kids would not be home until another hour so we knew we had the house to ourselves. And then
the phone rang.

I looked up at him and his eyes said don't worry about it, I won't
answer it. He held me tighter and kissed me deeper. The phone
caller decided to call again. I broke away from him with a hint of
disappointment and reached to answer the phone and I checked
the caller I. D. The number read Southlake Medical and I handed
it to him. He reluctantly took the phone, upset that our precious
time together was being interrupted yet again.

"Hello, this is Pastor Stevens," Lance said straightening up his clothes
as if the speaker could see him through the phone.

I patiently waited as I smelled his cologne upon my face from his
passionate kiss. I knew that our time together was over and I
glanced at the drawer that held my new lingerie and wondered if
we would find the time or the energy to enjoy some time together.

"Yes, maam. I wasn't aware that your son was in the hospital. Yes, I will be there in about an hour. I am so sorry and we will be praying for you. Yes, I will promise you that I will be there today."

I motioned to him about Junior's basketball game tonight and how he needed to go. I motioned like I was shooting a basketball hoping to remind him about his obligation to his children.

Lance looked up and shook his head and said into the phone. "Yes, Maam I will be there. Don't cry, sister, God knows what is best. Let's pray right now okay? Lord, watch over this sister and protect her child. We know that you know what is best for us."

As Lance prayed for this sister on the phone, I got from under his embrace and got out of the bed and walked to the restroom because I knew I would be going to another game alone. I freshened up my makeup and prepared to go to the kitchen to begin preparing dinner for my family. I walked by him as he was still praying for this woman and her son. I winked at him as I walked by to let him know that I enjoyed our little moment together. Later, Lance finished his phone call, cleaned and washed his car, showered and headed over to Southlake Medical. I watched him leave as I wrapped his plate of fried chicken, mustard greens, corn, sweet potatoes and peach cobbler and placed it in the refrigerator. I fed my children and I ironed Junior's uniform. On our way out of the door, Junior turned around and asked, "Mom is Dad going to be there tonight?" I looked at my fourteen year old who absolutely adored his Daddy and I said, "A member's son was critically injured in an accident today and he is with the family. I think he will be there if time allows." Junior just looked at me and gave a small smile and said "I will pray for that family that Dad is trying to help. I knew he was disappointed that his father may not be attending another one of his basketball

110

games, but he had developed a sense that his father was a hero who helped to rescue people. At the age of ten, Junior wrote a picture of a superhero with his father's face on it as a show and tell project in the fifth grade. And now I prayed that his hero would never disappoint him or let him down.

Chapter 14

The Game

We arrived to the Southlake High School ninth grade gym to find it packed with parents, fans and spectators. Junior's game would not begin until another thirty minutes. I watched as the Southlake cheerleaders performed their pre-game dance routine to pump up the crowd for the game. I spotted Deacon Jenkins in the stands and we walked over and sat by him. My girls, Connie and Jaylyn gave their customary hellos to Deacon Jenkins and lightly pecked him on each of his cheeks. It was times like this that I missed my father the most. My children did not have a maternal grandfather and Lance's father lives in Oakland, California but we rarely communicate with him.

"How are my precious angels doing today? How was school?" Deacon Jenkins asked Connie and Jaylyn.

"Fine" They both responded simultaneously as they both sat down beside him.

"Deacon Jenkins, I made an A on my math test today!" Connie excitedly told him.

"And I made an A+ on my science project" said Jaylyn trying not to be outdone by her younger sister.

"That is absolutely fantastic! I am so proud of you both" said Deacon Jenkins.

"You know, Deacon Jenkins, when I grow up I want to be a college professor just like you" said Connie.

"And one day you will teach at a college campus, I can just feel it in my bones," Deacon Jenkins said while juggling his body from side to side. Connie and Jaylyn both laughed hysterically.

"Look there is Daddy!" exclaimed Connie as she pointed across the gym. Lance was shaking a man's hand as he walked into the gym. He scanned the crowd, while the girls and I waved our hands to get his attention. He spotted us and coolly made his way over to us. His lean strides and confident gait let others know around him that he must be an important man. Lance greeted a few people in the stands and even stopped to talk to a young couple that I noticed he gave them his card. The girls and I waited patiently for him to sit with us in the stands before the game started.

"When is Daddy going to come and sit down with us? Its two minutes until game time" said Jaylyn. I watched my son practice and warm-up with his team. Lance had missed so many of Junior's games this season that Junior rarely scanned the crowd anymore looking for his Dad. I caught Junior's eye as he warmed up and I pointed in the direction of his Dad who was now shaking hands with Southlake's mayor whose son also played on the eighth grade basketball team. Junior looked and saw his Dad and nodded his head to acknowledge that he had spotted him. I breathed a sigh of relief that Lance had made it to Junior's playoff game in time.

About 10 minutes into Junior's basketball game, Lance finally made his way to the area where we were sitting.

"Man, I am beat from all that talking and politicking "Lance said as he plopped on a seat next to me, giving me a light kiss on the forehead. I politely looked away as if to say 'the king has arrived.'

"How is the Morris boy doing at Southlake Medical?" I asked Lance.

"Oh he is going to be just fine. He did break his wrist and has some scratches and bruises but it is a miracle that he is doing that well after being hit by that car." Lance said. "Babe, can you send them a card or bake them a cake of encouragement?" Lance asked.

"Yes, I'll make sure they get it by Tuesday. How are his parents doing?" I asked.

"They are both now calm knowing that their boy is going to be alright. Mr. Morris even said that he was going to visit our church this Sunday" Lance said to Deacon Jenkins and me. "Mrs. Morris is a six month new member of New Light but her husband hasn't been in church for over five years. Let's pray that this experience will bring him closer to God and the church."

Hey, Deacon Jenkins, thanks for taking care of my family while I was away" said Lance, giving Deacon Jenkins a firm handshake.

"Pastor, you know how I love you and your family, and we want to make sure you all are well taken care of, especially when the preacher is away" Deacon Jenkins said giving me a slight wink.

I suddenly felt a little uncomfortable and blushed. Lance looked at Deacon Jenkins and me and laughed. "Why Deacon Jenkins if I didn't say so, I think you might be flirting with my wife?" said Lance.

"Pastor, your wife could be my daughter and that is how I look at her, like a daughter. So as her father, I'm saying, you betta treat this gal right?" said Deacon Jenkins hitting Lance on the back with a playful left hook.

"Seriously, Deacon, I appreciate the way, you always look out for us and the way you look after my family. I've never had a chairman of deacons that cared for my family and I as you have. You are a blessed man, Jenkins," said Lance.

I looked at Deacon Jenkins and said, "Pastor is right, Deacon, we have never had a chairman that cared for us as much and we are both very grateful" I said hugging Lance around his waist and giving him a kiss on the cheek. "And Deacon Jenkins is right, Lance, you betta treat this woman right."

We watched the game. Junior scored twenty-one points, with six assists and five steals. Junior's team, the Southlake Cougars beat the Fourth Worth Tors, 62 to 59. It was a close game and Junior who plays point guard made the three point winning basket that put the Cougars on top! The fans went crazy at that last second three point shot! Junior was destined to be on the varsity basketball team by the time he reached his high school sophomore year. We celebrated by going out to eat at Thelma's Diner at Junior's request right after the game. I for one felt a little uncomfortable because I had just ate at Thelma's today for lunch with Deacon Jenkins and I hadn't mentioned to Lance that Deacon Jenkins and I had just "happened" upon Thelma's for lunch at the same time. God knows I hadn't done anything wrong and surely didn't have anything to hide. But I had learned as a pastor's wife that the "appearance" of things is very important. Any peculiar or odd moment can also get a person in trouble.

"Deacon Jenkins, won't you join us for a celebration dinner at Thelma's Diner tonight? My boy is the big man tonight and you are like family. Come on down and celebrate with us" said Lance.

"You, young folks go on and I'll see you all at church on Sunday. Besides, I had enough of Thelma's for one day. Her apple pie just tore up my stomach for lunch today, so I think I better settle for my sister Betty Jean's cooking tonight" said Deacon Jenkins. He quickly looked at me and I diverted my eyes.

"Okay, deacon, then we will see you on Sunday. You have a blessed weekend and tell Sister Betty I said hello and I am looking forward to eating one of her good ole fashion peach cobblers this Sunday after church" said Lance.

"I'll let her know that you hinted that you would like her to fix one of her cobbler dessert dishes" said Deacon Jenkins. "You guys have a nice celebration dinner," he said giving Junior a nice high five in the air.

"Thanks for coming to my game, Deacon Jenkins," said Lance.

"Sure son. You are a star in the making" Deacon Jenkins replied.

Deacon Jenkins walked past us, out through the gymnasium side doors.

"Thanks for coming Dad. I know you must be tired from your revival. I really am glad that you are here," said Junior as he walked up to his Dad to give him a hug.

Lance looked quite uncomfortable at this show of emotion from his son. He hugged him and replied, "I try my best to be here for you. I'm not too tired to be here for my boy! You played an awesome game. I am proud of you. You are representing the Stevens men well. And one day, you will grace the pulpit like the three previous Stevens men, your great grandfather, grandfather and your father before you and proclaim the good news of Jesus Christ.

Junior looked at his Daddy and replied his customary response that I had coached him to say whenever his father tried to push my son in the pulpit, "Whatever God wills me to do, Dad, I will do it," Junior responded. Junior was growing up with much wisdom. He knew it was better to just to give his Dad a response that was neutral. Because he was the only son of a pastor, persons in the church were always telling Junior that he would be a preacher one day like his daddy. Since the age of four, church women with their white gloves, would come by and pinch Junior's face as they passed by the communion table, and tell Junior, "Boy, you are going to be a preacher one day, just like your daddy." Little Junior would reeve back and just grin and say, "Whatever God wills." Those church women just loved his response and they would just chuckle and keep on walking as they shook hands with the other parishioners passing the communion table.

Later that night, we all went to Thelma's Diner. Lance was in a great mood. He was so excited that his son won a premier basketball game. As soon I walked in to Thelma's Diner, I noticed that Vivian Daniels was also at her sister's restaurant for dinner eating with one of her beauty salon operators. She looked at me and politely smiled and waved. I nervously waved back and sat Connie and Jaylyn down next to me at the table.

"Hey, babe, isn't that your beautician, Vivian Daniels over there?" Lance questioned.

"Yes, it is" I replied.

"Isn't she the one you said you had been trying to come and visit New Light for the last year? I hear that she can really make an organ talk and that she is really talented. Maybe I should go over and introduce myself and personally welcome her to New Light" Lance said.

"Sweetheart, we are here for Junior's game celebration. Can we just concentrate on him winning the game" I said as the children nervously looked at their father and I.

"I'm sure that you will have another time to talk to her about New Light. She is always in her cousin's diner and she is trying to enjoy her meal. Its 9:30pm and I can guarantee that girl has had a long hard day working at her salon" I said.

As soon as I sputtered out the words, Vivian got up from her booth and made an exit toward the door. However, before exiting, she politely made her way to our table. "Hello, Sister Stevens, and the Stevens children, and this must be Pastor Lance McClain Stevens. Hi, I am Vivian Daniels. Welcome to Southlake, Pastor" Vivian said with an outstretched French manicured hand. Lance shook her hand.

"Thank you, my sister. It is nice to finally meet you. I love the French roll that you gave my wife. I love to see her hair like that. You are mighty talented. I hope that you would be able to visit us one Sunday morning at the New Light church. I also hear that you are a great musician" said Lance.

"Why, yes Pastor. I enjoyed playing in the church for many years and I told your wife that I will try to make it to your first Pastoral appreciation service at New Light" said Vivian.

"Would you bless us with a solo on our appreciation 11:00 am morning service? I also hear that you can blow the roof off of a church with your eight octave range and that your range is so high that your voice never developed a falsetto. Is this true?

I wondered just how Lance knew so much about Vivian. I knew that she was a former musician but I didn't know that she had an eight octave range. I started to think that perhaps it his idea all along to get Vivian back into the church by telling me about her hair salon when we first moved to Southlake. I had told him only once that I had been trying to invite her to church. That is my Lance, always trying to get someone closer to Jesus.

"Pastor Stevens, you have heard a lot about me. Yes, I do love to sing and God has blessed both my sister Thelma and I with gifted voices and a gift of cooking. I will check my schedule and I will get back with you on that invitation to sing. It has been quite some time since I have sung or played in a church. But after seeing your Deacon Jenkins, here today at lunch with your first lady, it might just be time to visit New Light. That Deacon Jenkins doesn't look a day over fifty years-old" Vivian said with a gleam in her eye.

Lance immediately looked at me and raised his eyebrows and if to say, "Oh, really."

"I will let Deacon Jenkins know that you asked about him. And here is my card, feel free to contact me to let me know if you will be willing to sing. We are printing out the final programs this Thursday, so if you can please call me by Thursday morning I would appreciate it" Lance said.

"Yes, Pastor Stevens I will do that. You all enjoy your meal. Thelma's special tonight is fried catfish, collard greens, potato salad, baked beans, apple pie, and iced tea for only $4.99. It is absolutely delicious. Enjoy! Yawl, have a nice night" Vivian said and she strutted out of the door.

"You sure know a lot about Ms. Vivian." I said looking at Lance directly in his eye.

"And you sure know a lot about Thelma's Diner. Why didn't you tell me you had lunch with Deacon Jenkins today?" Lance quizzed. The waitress suddenly arrived to take our orders. We ordered our food and I carefully responded.

"I didn't have lunch or schedule a lunch date with anyone today Lance. I came here today for lunch and he was already here so we ate together. Remember, I said, leaning over to him, "I had planned a romantic morning with my husband who didn't make our date, so I did enjoy some company over lunch." I responded.

"You just have to be careful. We are still new to Southlake and you have to careful with the appearances of everything" he said.

"Yes dear. I have been a pastor's wife for over fifteen years so I am well aware of appearances. I was hungry, I came for lunch, Deacon Jenkins was here eating alone and so we ate together. You know that man is old enough to be my daddy, so why are you making a fuss about it" I responded.

"Well, the look he gave you at the game tonight, hmnn, he wants to be your Daddy, alright" Lance said looking away.

I smiled. "Is the great Lance Stevens a little jealous?" I asked.

He smiled at me and said, "Yes, I don't want anyone messing with my Goldie."

"Oh gosh, Mom and Dad" said Junior. "Please not at the table."

I think we forgot the children were within earshot.

"Mommy" said Connie with her big light brown eyes and long eye-lashes. "Who is Goldie?"

Lance and I looked at each other and burst into laughter.

"Sweetheart, Goldie is mommy and daddy's little secret. Now, finish eating your food" I said.

"I just notice that sometimes you call her Jackie and then some-times when you get that weird look in your eye, you call her Goldie. Is Mommy Goldie?" asked our curious eight year old.

Lance put his arm around my chair and said, "Yep, she is my Goldie. Go ahead little Connie do like your mama said and finish eating your food."

Lance ordered some wine to celebrate the win for Junior and he allowed the kids to take a sip in celebration. He began with a toast and said, "Did not Paul say that some wine is good for the stomach." I was just praying that no one from New Light entered at that moment to see their pastor making a toast in Thelma's Diner. I know we just had a discussion about appearances and here he is drinking some wine in public and with his kids. So much for appearances, I guess.

Later that night I wrote in my journal:

> Dear First *Lady,*
> *Today was an eventful day. My romantic morning with Lance was postponed. I had a nice lunch with Deacon Jenkins at Thelma's and I think Ms. Vivian Daniels has an eye on Deacon Jenkins. Junior won his game and he was great tonight. I am so proud of him. We still have yet to talk to his Dad about all of his extracurricular activities. I pray that Lance will listen to him. Our appreciation service is now a week away and I am getting nervous. Tomorrow, Lance is going to meet with dealers to purchase a 60 passenger bus for the church. He wants to start allowing his members to travel with him on his revivals. I need to schedule something productive to do while he is away. I will probably take the girls to the park or something. I was supposed to go to a mission meeting at the church tomorrow, but I think I am going to skip out on it tomorrow. I have been at that church at least six times this week and I need a break from it. May-*

be I will take Connie and Jaylyn to the movies as well. I just don't want to be stuck at the house doing housework all day because I know I will start snacking and eating too much. I learned today from Lance that the new member Marilyn Steele will start assisting the financial team at the church. She is rising up pretty fast in the church. She still avoids me for some reason. I hear she is quite good with finance books and she will be conducting internal audits on church finance and inventory records. She also sings in the choir and serves in the Women Ministry. She has been at New Light for only six months and she is already in positions of leadership. She even directed the youth choir last Sunday. And she finally stopped wearing the color red every Sunday. Lately she wears a white flower in her hair every Sunday. That girl, must be obsessive about clothes or something. I have noticed that she is quite friendly with Lance and some of the other men in the church. Sister Graves told me that Sister Steele has been calling Bro. Graves a lot lately just for counsel and advice. I suggested to Juanita that she pray over the situation before jumping to any conclusions. Juanita mentioned that Sister Steele is not close to any of the sisters in the church and is not looking for any type of womanly companionship. I prayed with Juanita on the phone and I shared with her a scripture in James, chapter 1, verse 2: "Consider it pure joy, my brothers, whenever you face trials of many kinds." I told her to keep praying for God's protection over their household and that this was a test of her faith. I am praying that I will have a discerning spirit to pray for others when they need it. Today was a good day and I am grateful to God for his blessings. Goodnight, First Lady...

Chapter 15

A Turn of the Tides

It was Sunday morning and it was a beautiful summer morning in Southlake, Texas. Lance was driving us to church this morning and talking on his cell phone. "Good Morning, Sister Steele, can you please bring a copy of last Sunday's financial records. I need to make a copy for our new trustee who has joined the staff." Lance paused for a few moments and then he said, "Yes, maam I did enjoy your chitlins you made last week and your 7-up cake was to die for. Thanks for sending it to Austin. There is nothing like a home cooked meal when you are traveling on a revival. Thanks again. We'll see you at church. Bye now."

I mysteriously looked over at Lance and raised my eyebrows.

"I forgot to tell you that some of the mission sisters sent up a plate of food to Austin for the revival" Lance said as he slightly tugged on his tie.

"You know those mission sisters never bother to call me to check on the kids and I, but they somehow manage to always send a gift to you during one of your revival trips. Did Sister Steele personally deliver the meal herself?" I asked with a tinge of anger.

"No, Jackie. Brother Jamison brought it to the hotel because he had a work related conference in Austin during the same week. So the missionary sisters asked him to bring it to me" Lance said.

"There is something strange, yet familiar about that Marilyn Steele lady. It's like I know her from somewhere. Yet, she avoids me every Sunday. Every time I try to speak to her, she purposefully walks away and she avoids direct eye contact with me" I said.

I noticed Lance looked uncomfortable and a few beads of sweat were appearing on his forehead. He raised the air conditioner in the car up to the highest level to bring in some more cool air. "You know, you need to give her a chance. She has not been in church very long and she is adjusting" Lance said.

"I know she has not been in church very long but she has propelled pretty fast at New Light. She was now directing the youth choir, serving as one of the financial secretaries, part of the mission Women's Ministry and the list goes on. She is learning fast, how to work in the church." I said. "Did you know that she has been spending a lot of time talking to your musician Brother Graves? So much so, that his wife Juanita called me last week and shared her personal concerns about it. She feels that it doesn't seem right that Sister Steele spends so much time talking to her husband on the phone and she refuses to even acknowledge Juanita" I said.

I knew Lance didn't like to talk about church gossip or mess on Sundays before he had to preach. So I knew he probably would not respond to my comments. We rode silently for the rest of the way to the church. New Light was approximately ten minutes from our house so it wasn't long before we were parking in Lance's parking space. We parked our Navigator next to Sister Finley's pink Cadillac.

It was 8:15am and we knew that the early bird saints had been at church since before 7:00am. There was talk about starting an early morning service since the 11:00am worship hour was packed now every Sunday. Lance was scheduled to meet with his board, elders and trustees about adding an additional worship time later on this week.

This Sunday kicked off our appreciation special services with the culmination on next Sunday at the 11:00am worship hour. We had a special guest preacher this morning coming from Chicago, Illinois. His name is Pastor Theodore Roosevelt. He and Lance met while attending seminary school. Pastor Roosevelt was now a senior pastor of a 2,000 member church right outside of Chicago. Deacon Jenkins had gone to pick him up from the airport at 8:00am this morning. Sister Finley and Sister Pepperdine were in charge of feeding the guest evangelist and the pastoral family. When we walked in the fellowship hall, Sister Finley was in the kitchen giving her customary orders to her committee and working with Sister Pepperdine to make sure the food tasted just right.

"Good morning, my Mary and Martha" Lance said jokingly to Sister Finley and Sister Pepperdine.

"How are you doing, Pastor. Good morning Sister Stevens. Why, I like that yellow suit and matching yellow hat you got on this morning. You look like the Queen of New Light!" said Sister Pepperdine.

"Thank you, Sister Pepperdine" I said.

Sister Finley walked out of the kitchen to give me a quick inspection. She looked me up and down and did not say a word but returned to the kitchen.

Lance noticed the awkward moment and quickly said, "Sister Finley, you and your team have done it again. These are some beautiful decorations. You all have done a superb job on creating an atmosphere of celebration."

The one thing I loved about my husband was that he knew how to encourage his church folks and get the ball rolling on a positive note. I decided that this was a perfect time to make an exit to the Pastor's study. I put my key into Lance's study and noticed that my key no longer worked on his door. Lance had given me a key to his office when we first arrived at New Light due to his important life insurance papers and he liked me to clean it up the way he preferred it. I quickly took my key out of the key hole and Sister Steele suddenly walked down the hallway and said, "Good morning First Lady, having trouble opening that door? Here let me open it for you." I stood back and was astonished to see that her key opened up my husband's office.

"There you go, First Lady. Your husband ordered all of the locks changed in the church two weeks ago, because so many members had access to the church and you know they updated the security system and only certain individuals now have access to church keys and the access code to the alarm system" she said as she straightened the white flower to perfection in her mid-length bone straight auburn blond streaked hair. She was wearing a pink pantsuit with a matching pink jacket that flared around her hips. Her three-inch white pointed Valerie Stevens shoes gave her a model type look that would make any man look twice at her. The pink in her outfit brought out her light brown skin and hazel green eyes. Sister Peterson had recently resorted to calling Sister Steele, "that yella' heifer with the green eyes." Sister Steele was indeed a beautiful woman and she used her beauty to gain influence and power wherever she went.

"I will make you another key to Pastor's office if you'd like?" she said with a smirk on her face. "I'll let Pastor know that you are waiting for him in his office" she said as she walked away.

Okay, what is she now. His personal secretary or what? This woman was rising up way too fast within New Light. I walked into the office and felt a pang of fear grip my body. Something was not right and my spirit was telling me to open up my eyes. How could this woman have a key to the Pastor's office? I walked into Lance's office and noticed that his entire office had been rearranged. The old burgundy plaid sofa had been replaced with a new leather full sofa, which apparently had a full size bed underneath. A new burgundy recliner was in the corner of his office and a new 52 inch flat screen TV laid fastened to his side wall and a new Mahogany five level bookcase, where all of his books were placed and stored under lock and key. His new office appeared to be a home away from home. I pray that the church purchased this new material because we didn't have any extra money to spend on this type of new furniture. After we pulled out of almost having to file for bankruptcy about five years ago, Lance allowed me to help him in managing our financial accounts and we promised never to purchase any major items unless we communicated about it first.

I was in pure amazement! Why didn't Lance tell me that he changed his office around? In the past, he always allowed me to help him rearrange his office or help him to get organized. I walked over to Lance's bathroom and twisted my church hat back to perfection and I applied more lipstick because my mouth went dry when I saw Sister Steele open up my husband's office and I assumed she was the one who rearranged his office as well. Who else could have done that?

I heard Lance enter his office talking to Deacon Jenkins on his cell phone. He walked in his office and exclaimed, "What the hell?" Oh excuse me, Deacon, but my office...someone has been in my office!" he said. Lance shook his head and continued, "Deacon, Pastor Roosevelt is about six feet tall, he is a dark skinned brother, with a gap in his mouth. You won't be able to miss him. If you still can't find him, have someone to page him in the airport. He didn't call to say he missed his flight or that he wasn't coming so I know he is there at the airport somewhere. Just try and look again. Thanks Deacon Jenkins. I will check the church's answering machine as well" Lance said as he sat down at his desk.

Sister Steele entered the office and went to the flat screen TV and turned it on.

"This is a surprise for you Pastor" she said. She looked at me, smiled and walked her little curvy tight pink pants suit out of his office.

Lance and I both gazed at the TV screen, which had a perfect picture of New Light's sanctuary. Apparently a new in-house TV security camera system had been installed as well. Lance was now able to view the sanctuary from his office. We watched as members came in and out of the sanctuary. I looked at Lance and he quickly looked away.

"Since when did you change the lock on your study and when did Ms. Thang, excuse me, Sister Steele, get a key to your office and did she also redecorate your office as well?" I carefully asked with a whole lot of sarcasm in my voice.

"Sweetie, can we talk about that later?"

Lance didn't know who had decorated his office or who installed the new camera system but he wasn't ready to tell Jackie that just yet, especially if she already knew that Marilyn Steele had a key to his office. Perhaps the TV, the new furniture was a gift to him for his appreciation celebration. He wasn't quite sure but he had to get out of this conversation and quick.

"I need to check my answering machine." Lance said. "I have an emergency going on right now. Deacon Jenkins cannot locate Pastor Roosevelt and his plane came in over an hour ago. I need to see if something came up with him. He is scheduled to preach this morning." Lance asked shuffling papers on his desk that I noticed was unusually very organized this morning, when most of the time he had papers scattered all over his desk.

"Who organized your desk? Did your new assistant finally get around to helping you with your office?" I asked.

"What, uh no" said Lance hastily apparently looking for Pastor Roosevelt's cell phone number. "I had to let her go before I left for Austin because she just wasn't working out. So, Sister Steele is helping me out for a couple of weeks until we can hire a new church secretary."

"Doesn't she already have a full time job serving as a corporate engineer at Verizon or something like that? How can she find time to be the church financial secretary and the church administrative assistant?" I said.

"Look! Can we talk about this at a later time!" Lance said looking me squarely in the eye with a hint of rage in his voice. "I have a dilemma going on right now and I need to focus, sweetie. Please, let's discuss this matter later on tonight" Lance stood up and walked around to the front of his desk. "Honey, would you please allow me to handle church business and give me some alone time right now?" Lance said. "I am at work."

It was more of a command than a question. I looked at him, grabbed my purse and bible and calmly walked out of his office. Out of the corner of my eye, I noticed Sister Steele leaning against the wall with her arms folded and a smirk on her face. Apparently, she might have heard our entire conversation. I really don't care what she heard. I still want to know why that yella heifer has a key to my husband's office and if she was behind redecorating his office. Something just isn't right.

Pastor Roosevelt walked into the pulpit exactly at 12:00pm. I could tell that Lance was furious that he was late to worship service. But of course, he gave his collegiate seminary buddy a grand introduction. Pastor Roosevelt preached on "Raise up his Arms" how Aaron and Hur raised Moses arms found in the bible in Exodus 17:12 which says: *When Moses' hands grew tired, they took a stone and put it under him and he sat on it. Aaron and Hur held his hands up—one on one side, one on the other—so that his hands remained steady till sunset.*

Pastor Roosevelt preached so hard that spit was coming out of his mouth, strands of sweat fell from his face and he began to sing-song the celebration part of his sermon. Brother Graves got on the organ and tuned up Pastor Roosevelt.

"And Aaron and Hur knew how to help the man of God. Can I get a witness? Tell me children, do you know how to help the man of God? Don't you know that when you bless the man of God, God will bless you! Don't you know that the Lawd is al---right! I---know he's alright! Yeesss he is! Can you say Yeah?" as he leaned back till it seemed his head would touch the floor. "Can you say Yeah?"

I watched the church roar in celebration. Sisters were passing out on the floor. Sister Finley had thrown her hat off so far that it slung into one of the church's side windows. Sister Pepperdine was dancing so hard in the middle isle that she lost both of her high-heeled shoes. Sister Marilyn Steele had completely passed out on the floor and a ton of male ushers rushed to her aid. I could hear her saying, before she fell out, of course, "Yes, Lord, I will help the man of God!" Sister Peterson who was sitting behind me in the pew, leaned forward and said, "Now, do you hear that mess! She needs to quit that. You betta watch that lady, she means us no good here at New Light." I quickly told Sister Peterson to be quiet.

By this time the church was on its feet and over ten people joined church as Pastor Roosevelt opened the doors of the church and sang the song, "I Won't Complain" made famous by the late Houston, TX, Pastor Paul Jones.

Everyone noticed that Sister Steele had miraculously come to herself and was now taking the information from the new members who accepted the invitation to accept Christ and become a member of New Light. Two or three women in the pews looked at me to say, "What is going on here?" I looked at them and smiled as if I knew exactly what was going on. I learned to never let church folks see me sweat. Not that Sister Steele was causing me to sweat any, but I was a little alarmed by her uncanny ability to be everywhere at the same time.

I couldn't help but notice how good Marilyn Steele looked standing next to my husband as he welcomed each new member to New Light. In fact, they made an attractive couple. They looked like the kind of ministry couple that you see on TBN or those other religious network stations. And to top it off, there seemed to be a certain chemistry between them that made me a little uncomfortable.

After church, Lance, Deacon Jenkins and Pastor Roosevelt went to lunch while the kids and I went home for lunch. We were scheduled to return to church at 4:00pm for the pre-appreciation service with guest church Pastor Wiley and the Mt. Olivet Church Family. After lunch, Junior begged me to stay home so that he could finish his science project that was due on Monday.

"Junior, why do you wait to the last minute to do everything?" I questioned. "You knew that we were having church today at 4pm. So I'm sorry son, you have to learn to prioritize. Your daddy is expecting you to play the drums for the youth choir when they sing this afternoon. Now, this is his special day. It wouldn't look right if you were not there."

"Yeah, you are right this is *his* day," said Junior under his breath.

"What did you say, young man?" I said stepping closer to him so that I was right under him. Junior had recently grown to at least 5'9" tall and with my frame of 5'5" I had to look up to him now.

"I said you are right it is *Daddy's* day. Did you see the program? New Light didn't even recognize us. Did you know that no one is on program to even talk about you? They have completely blotted you and the rest of us out, like Daddy is the only one they truly care about. They don't even have any reference to us, Mom. And I know Daddy sat quietly by and allowed them to do it. Doesn't he have the final say to what is on the program? Don't we sacrifice too, because we are in his family too? I may not be a preacher, but I know many times my daddy has chosen his church work over me. Last Friday, for example, was the first game my daddy has been to in at least a month and he never gets there on time!" Junior said as tears of frustration rolled down his face.

"I said I am not going to church. I'm working on my science project, so you can tell my Daddy that now I have more important priorities!" Junior ran to his room and shut the door.

Connie and Jaylyn ran from their rooms to see what the commotion was. "Mama, what is wrong with Junior? Why did he slam his door like that?" Connie asked.

"Junior just needs time to be alone," I said.

"I bet if Daddy were here, he wouldn't be slamming any doors," said Jaylyn with her hands on her little hips.

"Alright girls, go ahead and get dressed for service. Your dresses are ironed and are hanging up in your closets," I said.

"Is Junior going to church?" Jaylyn asked. "Because if he isn't going, I'm not going either," she said with her arms folded against her chest.

"Listen, missy, you go to that room and put those clothes on or I am not going to spare the rod on you," I told her as I inched closer to her with every word.

"Yes maam" Jaylyn replied. "I don't want to go to that stupid church anyway!" she stomped off.

Lord have mercy with me today. I grabbed the phone to call Lance and let him know what was going on with his son. I dialed his cell phone.

"This is Pastor" He answered.

"Lance, we have a problem. Junior won't come out of his room. He doesn't want to go to church today at 4pm because of his science project that is due tomorrow. What do you suggest?"

"Jackie, can't you handle that? I am trying to finalize some things for this afternoon program. Look, go put him on the phone. "

"Lance did you not hear me? He won't even open up his door and he is not coming out." I said with anxiety in my voice. "For years I have handled this family and there comes a point in life when a boy needs his father. Now, you need to get over here and talk to your child!" I screamed.

"I said I am busy and I need for you to take care of it" Lance said. "Hold on, Jacqueline."

I guess he thought he had put the mute button on the phone but he forgot.

"Yes. Thank you Sister Steele. These programs look great. I like the picture that you have of me on the front," I heard Lance say.

"Well, Pastor this is your special day and you deserve that and much more" responded Marilyn Steele, "Is there anything else I can do for you today?" she coolly asked.

At this point, I was boiling as I sat on the phone listening to everything.

"No, no you have done a fine job. Do you know who redecorated my office? I really like the new furniture and especially the new flat screen TV, are you behind this?" I heard Lance ask.

There was silence and I imagined Marilyn giving him her trademark smile. But there was no answer.

"Okay, I have Jacqueline on hold and I need to complete this call. Thank you very much, my sister" Lance said.

"Jackie, thanks for holding. Okay, listen I have some other business to attend to but let Junior know that if he is not here by 3:45pm I will personally see to it that he won't play in his next basketball game" Lance said.

"Lance, you and I both know that is not fair" I said.

"You heard what I said, and I mean what I say. I'll see you all at 3:45. Don't be late because you have to all sit together in the front pew" Lance said and he hung up the phone without saying good-bye.

Now at that very moment, I felt like taking off my clothes, and putting on some Texas spring clothes and taking my kids to the amusement park in Dallas, Six Flags over Texas. But I knew that wasn't the right thing to do. I walked to the breakfast area and nestled down at the prayer nook and began to talk to God.

Dear God,

I thank you for another day. I praise you for your awesome wonders. I magnify your name. Lord, create in me a clean heart. I confess any unpure thoughts, actions or feelings within my heart. Lord give me the spirit of David found in Psalm 51, for I know that is true biblical repentance. I stand on that Psalm right now, Jesus. Forgive me of my sins. Lord, I pray for my child Junior. Lord, you know this child better than I do. Give him what he needs to serve and worship you. Help him to learn to balance his school work and church life. Lord, help him to realize that he needs to be a good example for his little sisters. God, watch over my husband. Teach him how to prioritize his time with the church and the family. Help him to be a better father and watch over his children and be there for them even more. Lord, I thank you for my husband and my family. Help me to hold my tongue and give me what I need to be to my children when their father cannot be there. If it is your will, God bless us with prosperity, both spiritually, physically and in some ways materialistically. I stand on your word where you say, "You have not because you ask not." And Lord, right now I am requesting peace in my home.

Anoint my husband, give him joy to serve you even more. Bind the enemy from tempting my husband in any shape, form or fashion. Hold him in your palm of obedience. Lord, keep your Holy Ghost power around him. Father, help me to hold my tongue and to only speak of your praises. Lord, give me an unconditional love toward my husband even when I want to hit him on the head sometimes.

Help me to be an example of holiness so that others will see your light in me. I need you right now, Jesus. Expose and reveal to me my enemies. I know that we wrestle not against flesh and blood but against principalities, help me to realize that this battle will take much prayer and your power. Give me the strength to always assume the position of prayer, on my knees, to truly make it through this test and not try to do it on my own, without your guidance and protection. . I stand on your word in 2nd Corinthians 12:9 where you said, "My grace is sufficient for you, for my strength is made perfect in weakness." Help me, Lord. Bless this program today. Let your word be magnified in all we do. I love you, Lord. In Jesus name, let your will be done in our lives. I do pray this prayer, Amen.

I got off my knees, went to Junior's bedroom and told him his father's threat about not playing in the next basketball. As soon as I turned around, Junior came out, dressed in his Sunday suit and he made his way to the car. Connie and Jaylyn soon followed in their pink and green matching dresses with matching hat and gloves. They looked like little darlings. Their granny Eva Montgomery had those dresses mailed to them last week for this pre-appreciation service. I am really looking forward to seeing all of our relatives next week who will be in town to help us celebrate our 1 year appreciation here at New Light. I really need their presence and encouragement right now. My children and I drove in silence to New Light and arrived there at the church at approximately 3:45pm.

Chapter 16

The Kick-off Celebration:

The Pre-Appreciation Service

It was 4:10pm and the service still had not started. The church was packed with New Light and Mt. Olivet members who were greeting and hugging one another. The deacons came out at 4:15pm and started devotion, followed by Brother Marcus Graves and Genesis, his new Praise and Worship eight-member team, who ushered in a celebratory atmosphere of worship into the sanctuary. The choir did their processional to the choir stand, followed by the processional of deacons, deaconesses, preachers and pastors. I noticed that Marilyn Steele followed in after the pastors down the middle isle behind them. I couldn't tell if this was planned or if she just happened to be walking behind them. She marched up to the choir stand but she wasn't wearing a choir robe. She wore an elegant beaded off-white knee length dress with matching hat, shoes and purse. It accentuated her ample backside and small waist. The ushers led the children and me to our front row pew when we entered the church shortly before 4pm. Little eight year old Connie, nudged my side when she saw her daddy walk by during the processional, "Why didn't we walk with Daddy down the aisle this year?"

"Because it was not necessary this time," I said.

"Daddy, doesn't love us anymore? Is that why he didn't want us to walk with him?" she continued to ask.

"No, it's because New Light doesn't like us anymore. We are just part of Daddy's package that's all," Jaylyn said.

I turned around and told both of them to behave and be quiet. It bothered me that Jaylyn would say something like that to her little sister. And since when did she think we were a package? That girl must have been watching too much television again or overhearing the conversations of adults. I prayed daily that my children were not emotionally disturbed by some of the comments that they may have overheard in the church.

The congregation sat down after the processional and the ministers conducted pulpit devotion. I noticed Mt. Olivet's First Lady, Sister Patricia Wiley sitting over in the fourth pew with a red pearl beaded hat and a red and white suit. She looked absolutely beautiful. I wondered why the ushers did not seat her next to me. I specifically asked all of the ushers to sit any visiting minister's wife on a pew with me. I remembered that Lance had to have a protocol session with the ushers to share with them his seating preferences and the type of drinks that he needed for his throat along with air conditioning concerns over the pulpit. All New Light's and visiting ministers' wives or deacons' wives were to be escorted to the first two pews on the right. At that moment, Sister Wiley caught my gaze, I mouthed "hello" and she quickly looked away without even speaking to me in response.

Okay, I thought to myself. What is up with her?

Our new and improved 52-member choir brought the house down by singing Israel and New Breed's single, "We Worship You," and the Luke Mercer Jr. & Chosen title cut, "My New Life." The church was on fire! Brother Marcus Graves and his wife Juanita led a duet together singing a melody of hymns, which included, "Blessed Assurance," "He Looked beyond My Faults," "Oh Sweet Jesus" and "I Must tell Jesus." It was awesome! Juanita belted out her customary first Soprano and brought the church to tears as she sang while playing the piano and Brother Graves was making that B3 Hammond organ talk!! They ended their song service with national gospel artist Houstonian Kathy Taylor Brown's song, "Come Let's Worship the Lamb of God."

Afterward, Deacon Finley was listed on the program to talk about his Pastor as a leader. But instead of Deacon Finley getting up to speak, Sister Marilyn Steele took the podium.

She straightened out her pearl beaded white dress, which was by the way, the same color dress that I had on, and cleared her throat.

"As you can see, I am not Deacon Finley," she said as the congregation chuckled. "But it was determined at the last minute, with the pastor's permission of course, that a man and a woman should speak about our great pastor."

"Amen," said some of the people in the pews. "Alright…say that."

"Giving praise to God, in respect to the pulpit, to our honoree, and my brothers and sisters in Christ, Pastor Lance McClain Stevens is an awesome man of God. I have only been a member of this great fellowship for the last six months. Within those months I have seen this church grow tremendously. We average about 10 people joining our church per month. We purchased a new church 57-passenger charter bus on yesterday. So, get ready New Light, we will be on the road in our new 57-passenger bus traveling with our pastor as he preaches on the road," Marilyn said.

The choir has new robes and a great musician in Brother Graves," she said with a huge smile on her face and nodding to Brother Graves on the organ.

Everyone noticed how Sister Steele just ignored Juanita Graves or forgot to mention her name as part of the musical team. I looked at Juanita who was sitting on the piano, who just kept her chin up looking at Marilyn Steele.

Marilyn continued with much confidence.

"Pastor Stevens is an astute business man who knows how to conduct the Lord's business with professionalism and accuracy. He established a 501©3 Community Development Corporation which created Victorious Workers, a Christian Temporary Agency. He also created at least four new ministries in his first year tenure at New Light. As a matter of fact, he has just appointed me, Women Ministry Coordinator here at New Light by the recommendation of Deaconess Sarah Finley who will be stepping down as Coordinator at the end of the year" Marilyn said with a smile to Sister Finley.

I noticed Sister Sarah Finley out of the side of my peripheral vision look straight at me with a smile on her face as if to say, "I finally got you!"

I wished I could have knocked that purple hat off of her head right at that moment. I definitely needed to go home and meditate on Psalm Chapters 55 through 57 concerning my enemies. I needed to call out Sister Finley by name when I read those scriptures.

"Pastor is taking our church to a new level in Kingdom Building!" Marilyn exclaimed, her voice rising with each new sentence. "He is a community builder serving on two Ad-Hoc committees in Southlake. His sermons are clear, plain, and yet thorough. He teaches us to understand the scriptures not only for content but for context and historical purposes as well. He averages at least 50 people a week in his bible study classes. And our church school has grown to over 100 class enrollees! Lance, …uh, oops, excuse me; Pastor Stevens is a great friend, confidante, counselor and father to his children. When I joined New Light I was desperate for deliverance, in more ways than one. Pastor Stevens delivered me toward the light of Jesus! And I am going to follow him for the rest of my life!"

I looked over at Lance who was sitting on the side of the pulpit in a kingly chair that was purposefully decorated in purple and gold. He began to shift in his seat as Sister Steele continued to talk. He had his chin up looking toward her with this weird expression on his face like he was somewhat confused. Lance returned my gaze and I slyly rolled my eyes away from him as if to communicate to him, "Whatever!"

"I have known Pastor Stevens since the age of eight when I would visit my grandmother in Houston, TX" Sister Steele continued with a dreamy expression upon her face like an obsessed woman.

"And I must say he has turned into a great man and fine pastor. I am very proud of you Pastor Lance McClain Stevens. I always knew that you would make me, I mean us proud. I love you, Lance,..oops.. uh.. forgive me, Pastor Stevens. Let's give it up for our Pastor!" she said as she began to clap her hands.

She then walked down from the podium and proceeded to walk over to Lance and have him a quick kiss on his lips and a big bear hug. Lance looked at her quite awestruck, and obviously hoped that no one had seen her quick brush across his lips as she hugged him. But she positioned herself to where only the first three rows of people on her right could see it. I saw it all and so did dear old Sister Peterson and Juanita Graves. Marilyn Steele turned, looked at me, smiled and took her seat behind the pulpit in the choir stand.

As the people were clapping for their beloved pastor and Sister Steele's sincere expressions, Sister Peterson threw up her hat from her head across the church where it landed in the center aisle and screamed, "Oh Lord!" and she passed out on the pew behind me. I turned around and motioned for the ushers to escort her out. When she came to herself after about 10 seconds, she hollered "Why, Jesus, Why?" as the ushered carried her out. She began to sing her familiar code word song.

I don't know what Jesus is to you. But I hope He is to you what He is to me.

I could tell that some people were uncomfortable with Sister Steel's familiarity with their pastor and to think she called him by his first name twice. They knew that I didn't even call him by his first name at church. I genuinely displayed respect for him and his position and called him Pastor around his members. And I rarely kissed him on the lips at the church in front of parishioners. This woman was bold and she didn't seem to care who knew about her affection for her pastor.

Lord have mercy! Well I couldn't clap in jubilee because I was stunned. Lance already knew this woman, yet he never told me that he already knew her!! Now, that was something that needed to be investigated further. I could tell that there were some people who were looking a little concerned as well. Sister Steele didn't even use a Bible verse in her talk about her pastor and then she had the nerve to say 'I love you, Lance.' *Okay, calm down, Jackie or else you may find yourself on the front steps of this church fighting Lance, Sister Steele, and probably Sister Finley, too.* I imagined myself getting my Bible, slapping him, knocking Sister Steele out with the back side of my Bible, and karate kicking Sister Finley with a round away right foot kick all in the name of Jesus of course.

I wanted to let them all know that Jacqueline Renee Stevens is not to be played with. First Sister Steele disrespected me by avoiding me every Sunday, then she sarcastically opened the door for me to my husband's office when she knew I didn't have a key, she snickered by his office upon hearing our slight discussion, and finally she let's me know publicly that she had known my husband longer than I had and they had a history together which I knew nothing about. I assumed that Sister Finley cleverly deleted the pastoral family from the appreciation service and she is probably the culprit who convinced Sister Steele to have a speaking part on the program. Deacon & Sister Finley were the chairpersons of the Appreciation Ministry Celebration. Yet, wasn't my husband, Lance the pastor and didn't he have to approve all of this? Upon this realization, my heart sank and I wiped away a small tear that crawled its way out of the corner of my eye.

Deacon Finley took to the podium to talk about his Pastor as a shepherd, but I was in a daze and I couldn't even tell you what he said about Lance. I wanted to grab my purse and get the hell out of that church, but I decided to be the regal queen that I am and I stayed glued to my seat with a smile on my face. I watched the festivities continue. Everyone raved about their new fresh pastor who had a vision for the people of New Light and the community of Southlake.

Pastor Wiley preached a sermon on learning to be content in whatever state we are in. His wife, Sister Patricia Wiley, who was now only singing gospel songs and not her customary R&B lyrics that some folks would hear at Southlake's *The Back Door Club.* She sang a song by Yolanda Adams called, "In the Midst of it All," during the invitational period when Pastor Wiley was calling for sinners to be saved and saints restored. Now, Sister Wiley may have talked a lot but she sure could sing. There was something in her eyes when she sang that let me know she was battling something deep within. She wasn't able to finish her song, because of her tears. A Mt. Olivet usher led her outside of the sanctuary to the women's restroom. I thought this might be a good time to talk to her. I followed them to the women's restroom.

"Sister Wiley, are you okay?" I asked giving her a hug.

"Yes. I am," she said, dabbing her eyes with a Kleenex. Her eyes were red and she removed her hat. "Sister Stevens, I want to thank you for the advice you shared with me about my tongue. You were so right. I am having a horrible time adjusting to being a pastor's wife. I am so unhappy. I'm still learning how to be a good wife and then with the addition of having the scrutiny of being a Pastor's wife. It's a bit much. Everything I do is under a microscope. It's like I am supposed to be superhuman or something. I know I need Jesus. I wasn't going to church like I needed to when I met Pastor Wiley. I finally figured out that everything I shared at Heavenly Hands Beauty Salon, Vivian Daniels and her crew went around town telling everyone what I told them. Now, I do my own hair and I am looking for a new beautician. And my Wiley seems to give all of our money to the church. A member needs a bill paid or a child has an emergency and they come to us. Well I'm tired of giving all of my money away to his members and then they treat me so cruel. We tithe and give offerings, shouldn't that be enough? And then the church let Wiley's health insurance lapse by mistake and now we have to pay a $2,000 medical bill of his from last month. I am just sick of it all. I feel that God played a trick on me or something. I thought being a Pastor's wife was a glamorous life. I loved the way I would see preachers' wives strut in their suits and hats with a joyful smiles on their faces. But how can you be joyful on this journey? All of these expectations! Go to Sunday school every week, bible study, choir rehearsals, youth meetings. The next thing they are going to want me to do is to be a janitor or an usher. I can't serve the Lord with gladness if I am always trying to please these folks," she cried.

"Stop trying to please those folks and learn to please God and realize that in your serving God you will offend some people. But still count it all joy! You have got to be delivered from being a people pleaser," I told her as I hugged her. "In order to have joy in this life, you must concentrate on Jesus. The J in joy stands for Jesus! The minute you take out the *J* in the word joy, then all you have left is the *OY*. Then you will find out that you have the *Oh Why Me Syndrome*. Why is this happening to me, Lord? Why are the members treating me so bad? What have I done? You must focus on Jesus to have real joy."

I looked her straight in her eye. "Get into the Word of God and study His Word. Your songs will take on new meaning when you have the word of God in your heart. This life doesn't get any easier but you have got to find positive ways to cope with the pain. Pray more, run to exercise off some steam, take a walk around the block; but being in a pity party will only lead you into the throngs of a deep depression. You have to find positive methods of coping in this life. Paul said that in whatever state he was in he learned to be content. You've got to seek holiness in this life to truly be happy. Focus on being the best Christian you can be and everything else will fall into place," I assured her.

"Girl, you are not fighting people, you are fighting evil spirits and principalities. Don't you know the demons rose up the minute you walked into that church? They recognize the gifts and the purpose that God has for you and they are determined to cause you to stumble and cripple your Christian walk. You have got to put on the whole armor of God if you are to survive in this life. Stop looking with your physical eye but see the Christian fight with your spiritual eyes," I ministered to her.

Sister Wiley leaned against me and cried and for a moment I forgot about my own troubles and the hurt I was feeling because my husband had not disclosed certain information concerning Marilyn Steele.

We rocked together on the love seat in the ladies bathroom. I locked the door forcing other parishioners to use the women's restroom in the front of the church. We prayed together and I helped her readjust her makeup. I helped her with her hat and noticed that her short bob was actually a weave that needed some attention. I told her to reconsider about not going back to Heavenly Hands and

148

learn not to allow Ms. Vivian or her patrons to pick her for information anymore. But if she couldn't resist talking about her issues then perhaps she needed to go to a salon where the people didn't know her that well. But by the looks of her weave, she needed to go to somebody's salon and quick!

We promised to keep in touch and become prayer partners. We waited until the benediction was over and the church members dismissed and we returned to the sanctuary. I noticed that Marilyn Steele was standing by my husband and greeting visitors and members as if she was the pastor's wife. When she saw me walking toward them, she politely excused herself and walked away. She walked by me and didn't even say hello. Well, I didn't bother to speak either, so the feeling was mutual. I did see her trademark smirk upon her face as she passed by me and I raised my chin higher as I walked toward my husband and Pastor Wiley.

I walked up to stand beside Lance and Sister Wiley gave Pastor Wiley a hug for a great sermon. I heard him tell her that she blew the roof off with her song, "In the Midst of It All." I could tell that they both really cared for each other.

"Hey Goldie. You are looking mighty fine in that white dress. Is that the one I bought you from Neiman Marcus from the Houston Galleria?" Lance asked me.

"No, it isn't," I calmly replied. "This is the one you bought me from Kmart," I said loud enough so Pastor and Sister Wiley could hear me. They both looked at me and lowered their eyes.

"Girl, you are such a jokester," Lance said looking at me uncomfortably. I looked at him as if to say, "Yeah, Negro, you got some explaining to do."

"Pastor Wiley, please follow me to my study and we will give you your love offering and then have dinner in our fellowship hall," Lance said.

"Pastor Wiley and Sister Wiley thank you so much for coming today. I will talk to you soon."

I walked coolly away. I retrieved all of my children; I got in my car and went home. I didn't want to fellowship with anyone and I knew that my absence in the fellowship hall for dinner might cause some eyebrows to rise, but at that moment I really didn't care what anyone thought. I would not allow Lance to take this family for granted and so he could see how it felt when we were absent. It would cause him to look a little shady or not as perfect as he tried to make us all look for "appearances sake".

I am sure they all had a nice fellowship dinner. My children were happy to be home early and it allowed Junior enough time to work on his science project before bed. I took off my Neiman Marcus dress, put on my familiar cotton pajamas and retrieved a Snicker's Ice Cream Bar from the freezer and snuggled down to watch a good chick flick on Lifetime Cable for Women.

Chapter 17

The Confrontation

I awoke to a sound at the foot of my bed. I opened my eyes to see my husband Lance pulling off his shoes at the edge of the bed. I looked at the alarm clock and it read 11:15pm. I wondered to myself where had he been for the last few hours. I exhaled to let him know that I was up and it was time to talk about today's events. I leaned up on one elbow and said,

"When were you going to let me know that you personally knew Sister Marilyn Steele? And how does she get a new key to your office before me? And why did she walk down the middle aisle with the preachers? And when did she get so comfortable with you that she can kiss you on your lips? Is she your whore now? What is going on Lance? It just doesn't look right! And the Spirit of the Lord is telling me that something is not right."

By this time I was standing up on the side of the bed with my hands on my hips and my French roll purple wrap on my head. I wanted to know what was going on and I wanted to know right then.

"I am tired right now and I don't want to talk about it. Yes, babe I know it looked odd. I'm trying to figure it all out too. I am just exhausted right now," Lance said.

I could see the exhaustion in his face but I didn't care. It was time to communicate and I wouldn't wait until *he* was ready.

"You come home at 11:15pm don't even call and say that you are going to be late and then you stroll up and say you don't want to talk about it? Did you come home late on purpose so you wouldn't have to talk about it?" I screamed.

"If you must know, I have been at the hospital with one of our new members, Justin Brown, who is suffering from a diabetic coma. The boy is 19 years old and I've been at the hospital with the family for the last two hours, praying and ministering to them," Lance said. "Sweetie, I am tired right now. I know we need to talk, but please I am too tired to talk tonight. I was hoping that I could fall asleep in your arms but I guess that is out too," he said.

"Yes, you guessed right because Goldie is out of commission until you and I communicate," I quipped and folded my arms across my chest.

"You know the Bible says in 1st Corinthians 7: 5, that you cannot withhold from me unless we both consent for a time," Lance said using one of his favorite Bible quotations to hook me in.

"Your coming home after 10pm without a phone call is enough consent, so since you can't respect Goldie, you can't have Goldie," I said. "Matter of fact, you can't even sleep with Goldie. So I advise you to go and sleep in the guest room until you are ready to communicate," I said without backing down.

"Are you serious? Jackie, please" Lance begged. "Well, this is my house, my bed and I am going to sleep in it tonight," said Lance.

"No Lance! First of all, this is not *your* house. It is New Light's house. Remember that. We don't own a home. I am tired of you taking me for granted and I am always playing by your rules. This time I need to talk to you and ask some questions and I don't want to wait until tomorrow," I said.

I was totally ticked off because he didn't even ask me why we didn't come to the fellowship hall to have dinner with him. He seemed so unconcerned about us that I wondered if he even noticed that we weren't there. This time he was going to talk to me or face the consequences.

"Lance, talk to me!" I screamed.

"Why won't you talk to me? I want to talk about what happened to-day right here, right now!" I said with my hands on my hips and my neck seemed to be doing loops.

As soon as I said that, I felt so childish. Now at 39 years old, I felt like I was acting like a 22-year-old newlywed.

"Okay, fine, fine Lance. You win. We can talk about this tomorrow or whenever you are ready," I reluctantly relented. "I am going out to take a walk. I just need some air."

I put on my gym shorts, tennis shoes and a light shirt and headed downstairs. I needed to walk or else I would eat and I knew that was a bad habit that wouldn't help me to cope well with this dilemma.

"Honey, wait, its too late at night to be walking by yourself," Lance said.

"Then come with me," I said knowing that he was too lazy and tired to follow after me.

I walked and then power walked around our neighborhood. I felt much better afterwards and it allowed me to think and calm down. I knew I might be a little tired at work the next day but I needed to relieve my stress. I truly enjoyed walking because it also allowed me to talk to God. I prayed that God would help me deal with my anger issues and to reveal to me the truth about this Marilyn Steele woman. As I walked, I prayed for protection over my husband, that he would not fall into temptation. I was in fact prayer walking over my situation. I wanted to make sure that Satan would not penetrate into my marriage or into my spirit. I truly believe that it is through praise and worship that we can receive our breakthrough. While I walked I recited Psalm 91, a passage that I had memorized over time to speak strength into my spirit.

Psalm 91:

He who dwells in the shelter of the Most High
will rest in the shadow of the Almighty

I will say of the LORD, "He is my refuge and my fortress,
my God, in whom I trust."

Surely he will save you from the fowler's snare
and from the deadly pestilence.

He will cover you with his feathers,
and under his wings you will find refuge;
his faithfulness will be your shield and rampart.

You will not fear the terror of night,
nor the arrow that flies by day,

Nor the pestilence that stalks in the darkness,
nor the plague that destroys at midday.

A thousand may fall at your side,
ten thousand at your right hand,
but it will not come near you.

You will only observe with your eyes
and see the punishment of the wicked.

If you make the Most High your dwelling—
even the LORD, who is my refuge-

Then no harm will befall you,
no disaster will come near your tent.

For he will command his angels concerning you
to guard you in all your ways;

They will lift you up in their hands,
so that you will not strike your foot against a stone.

You will tread upon the lion and the cobra;
you will trample the great lion and the serpent.

"Because he loves me," says the LORD, "I will rescue him;
I will protect him, for he acknowledges my name.

He will call upon me, and I will answer him;
I will be with him in trouble,
I will deliver him and honor him.

With long life will I satisfy him
and show him my salvation."

It took me about four years to memorize the entire passage of Psalm 91 but I determined that I would hide God's word in my heart that I would not sin against God. I knew that my flesh is weak and naturally contrite. I needed to get this scripture in my spirit to know that the battle is truly not mine but it is the Lord's! I learned a few years ago by reading Cindy Trimm novel, *The Rules of Engagement* that I am to position myself to war in prayer to cover over the situations in my life that try to separate me from God. I remember a time, when I would get all up in Lance's face with my concerns and demand that he communicate. I had learned over time that it only tired me out from huffing and puffing and so began to cool my steam by prayer walking. Lance knew that if I was out walking then I was praying over our family and our current situations. He would often tease me and say, "Man, I couldn't get away with anything if I wanted to. My wife has me covered in so much prayer that I'm afraid if I even thought of something lewd, the Holy Ghost would knock me out."

I know that I can't change any man, but I serve a God that can change any person, thing, creature or law and that is My Jehovah, God who has all power in His hands. I nurtured a personal relationship with God about five years ago. I was brought up in the church all of my life and had long since accepted Jesus in my heart. But it wasn't until about the age of 32 that I really began to know the person of God. Jesus became my best friend. He truly began to talk to me in ways that I had never heard before. But it was only after I truly began to read His Word, fast and meditate upon it. I still try to fast at least once a week so that I can effectively hear from God.

My feet were beginning to get sore as they pounded upon the pavement. In my haste, I forgot to put my socks on with my tennis shoes.

156

Beads of sweat began to form around my forehead. I kept walking and I kept walking until I felt a blister pop under my foot. I knew I had probably power walked for about 4 miles because it was now 1:15am in the morning. I continued until I reached our home and I stood on the front lawn and looked up into the sky to feel the radiance of the moonlight upon my face.

"Oh, God, you are my refuge and my strength," I said out loud. "Now lord, my head says to wake up that man in there and give him a piece of my mind, because he needs to talk to me. But I need you Lord, to calm my spirit. I want to be a woman who builds up my house and not one who tears it down. I am still angry because that fool let me walk out here by myself and it's past 1:00am in the morning. Lord, doesn't he care for my safety?"

A small gentle wind passed over my face and I heard a still small voice within my spirit say, "You chose to go walking at this time of morning and so you compromised your own safety. You can't blame him for your own choices."

I silently laughed to myself. My God has a sense of humor and I knew that it was His voice that I had heard. I quickly walked into the house, silently went upstairs to our bathroom, showered, and returned to my husband's side underneath our covers of safety and warmth.

Lance turned over and put his arm around me and I snuggled under his embrace. I exhaled and prayed that a new day would bring new mercies as I fell asleep in my husband's arms.

Chapter 18

Good Gossip

"Chile, did you see that woman kiss Pastor Stevens on the lips?" asked Kayla, Sister Finley's niece.

"Naw, girl, I guess from where I was sitting I didn't see it. It must have been quick," said Sister Pepperdine. They were both enjoying a Monday brunch in the home of Sister Finley.

"Auntie Sarah, what do you think about what happened at church yesterday?" Kayla asked her aunt.

Sister Finley brought their coffee to the table and calmly sat down. "I think the young woman really cares for our Pastor and she wants to do whatever she can to help our great church."

"I can't believe Sarah that you are not going to lead the mission group or Women's Ministry anymore. You have led that ministry for over 20 years," Sister Pepperdine said.

"I think its time for new leadership within our church and I am not getting any younger, just better" snickered Sister Finley. "Besides, Marilyn Steele and Pastor Stevens look good together. They are a strong power couple and the look for leadership to represent New Light," said Sister Finley.

"But Auntie, Pastor Stevens has a wife and so," Kayla said carefully.

"And so?" responded Sister Finley

"And you shouldn't try to put someone between a man and his wife" said Kayla. "Auntie, that is a sin against God and I know that Jacqueline Stevens is a praying woman. You go around and meddle around with her and find yourself sick or something."

"Oh, please. I have been around New Light long enough to see many things and the handwriting is on the wall that this Marilyn Steele is going to be the next Mrs. Lance McClain Stevens. Our preacher is not strong enough to stop the advances of a beautiful woman like that. Hey, I keep reminding Abraham from looking at the woman too hard on Sundays and I for one wasn't so happy when she became the deacon's financial secretary. However, I have formed an allegiance with her and so now we are friends."

"Do you really think that she may be the next Mrs. Stevens?" Sister Pepperdine asked as she leaned against the table. "Well, Sarah you said that about our last Pastor too and you were right."

"What!! I just heard that happened with our last Pastor and I didn't think it was true. These preachers today, need to stop judging others so hard and start living the life of a saint. If it is not money that tempts them, it is another woman," said Kayla shaking her head.

"And in some circles, its little boys too!" hollered Sister Pepperdine as they all leaned back in their chair with laughter.

"Satan is just having a field day with men of the cloth. Auntie, is it really true that our last pastor at New Light, Pastor Stewart, had two children with a woman that is not his wife. Is that true? Is she from Southlake?" asked Kayla.

"I don't think you know her Kayla. She was from Houston or something like that," said Sister Finley with a sudden look of disinterest on her face.

"Yes, I heard in the beauty shop a couple of months ago that her name is Mona, , LaMonica, uh…Monique Howard or something like that. Yes, that's her name, Monique Howard," said Sister Pepperdine looking up into the air trying to recall the name she had heard in the beauty salon. "And she isn't from Houston Sarah, she is from Dallas," she continued looking at Sarah strangely, who was now shaking her head and lowering her eyes to the floor so that Kayla couldn't see her expression.

Kayla looked at her Aunt Sarah and knew that something wasn't quite right. "That's funny," Kayla said. "We have a cousin named Monique Howard who lives in Dallas. She used to stay in Abilene, Texas. Hmnn. That's odd. I just saw her about three weeks ago at the mall and she told me she was eight months pregnant. Somebody is sure enough taking care of her because she was sporting a huge ring on her finger."

"Do you all need some more coffee?" Sister Finley interjected quite oddly. "I just bought this imported coffee last week and it is absolutely delicious. "

"Wait a minute, Auntie, is this our distant cousin, our 3rd cousin, Monique Howard from South Oakcliff that had those two babies by our last Pastor? Monique Howard with the coca cola bottle shape and booty for days that can make a strong man weak? Monique Howard with the naturally curly jet-black hair that falls to her shoulders! Everyone knows that Monique and her mama, Janie Sue are convention and revival whores and natural born gold diggers! Their reputation is known from Galveston to El Paso, TX within the church circuit!" Kayla said looking at her favorite Auntie like she was stone crazy.

"Auntie!" exclaimed Kayla rising up from her seat. "Did you have anything to do with helping to break up that man's marriage? I remember how you couldn't stand Pastor Stewart."

"What?" said Sister Finley with a look of guilt all over her face.

"I didn't break up anybody's marriage. Their marriage was already broken when they first came to New Light. Monique just needed a place to live because her mama would always bring different men in the house, so I helped her to relocate to Abilene. I couldn't have anyone in Southlake knowing that we were kinfolk. Her mama was too busy chasing this married minister to do anything to help her own child. So, I had to help Monique. That girl's reputation and her mama's past would ruin my good reputation in Southlake. Pastor Stewart was doing a revival in Abilene and I asked him to stop by and pray with her because she was in a strange place with no family members near by. She was only 25 years old at the time and she needed some guidance and I for one was tired of always coming to her rescue and giving her money every other month."

"You knew that Monique would freely give her body to any man who was a preacher or a blue collar $80,000 a year plant man. All she sees is money, power and prestige. Monique is a wounded soul who is looking for love in all the wrong places. How could you Aunt Sarah?" Kayla accused with tears in her eyes.

"Did I put a gun to his head to sleep with that woman? Did I tell him to go and have two babies with that woman?" replied her Aunt Sarah with anger in her voice.

"He should have known to take a deacon or another witness with him to go see her. So don't go blaming me for Pastor Stewart's weaknesses" responded Sister Finley with her arms folded against her chest and her chin up in the air. "Monique did call me for some money and counsel so I sent Pastor Stewart by there to drop off some money and to pray with her when he was in Abilene for a revival. How was I to know that fool was going to fall for her tricks?"

"No you didn't put a gun to his head, Auntie. You did however set him up to meet a very aggressive man hungry, beautiful young girl who you knew was poison and used goods. And you probably didn't warn him about her either. You won't even let your own husband step within two feet of Monique or Janie Sue. You know that Monique has issues ever since she was date raped at the age of fifteen and you paid for her abortion. You pretty much excommunicated them from the family after that. Yeah, you didn't know I knew about the abortion, but she told me. Janie Sue had a field day telling some of the family members at our last family reunion that 'if you were such a Christian then why did you pay to have her grandbaby killed?' She also said that we shouldn't judge her for just *spending time* with her preacher friends, when you are out committing murder and setting up evil traps for preachers," Kayla said with her arms outstretched in the air.

"I thought Janie Sue was out of her mind or perhaps just extremely jealous of you. "How could you Auntie? You are not a Christian, but just an example of "church folk" who do not know Christ, but only want power and control for themselves and use the church as a game or a tool for their own agenda and vain glory," said Kayla.

Sister Finley sat straight up in her chair and looked over at Kayla squarely in her eye, "Now you listen to me, nobody is going to set foot in my house and disrespect me; especially not some 25-year-old young girl like you, who I practically raised and sent you to college because your poor mama and daddy couldn't do it. So, you hush your mouth right now and stop all this foolishness. You don't know what I have had to do to protect the dignity of New Light and our good family name. Monique and her mama Janie Sue had always used me to get them out of trouble.

Kayla looked at her aunt and quietly sat down at the table. The silence that followed was deafening.

Sister Pepperdine looked at her lifelong friend Sarah Finley and wondered how she could try to set up the man of God. She silently shook her head.

"Don't you look at me like that Betty Jean Pepperdine!" shouted Sister Finley

"Don't you sit there and judge me. You sat with me and talked about Pastor Stewart and his wife like a dog as well. Nodding your head and laughing with me. And silence is agreement isn't it Betty Jean?"

"Sarah, if I laughed it was because of all the information you were telling me about them. I didn't think it was true, but to try to set up the man of God and to destroy a family. Well, that is going too far. Even I know the Bible says, 'Touch not my anointed.' It's a wonder you haven't ended up sick or worse. You can't play with the man of God. You have let the enemy use you in a mighty way. And you paid for a teenager to have an abortion? You helped to kill a child! Sarah, you are supposed to be a Christian woman. You are supposed to believe that nothing is too hard for God," said Sister Pepperdine as she looked at her friend in a new light. "You always told me that you were a pro-lifer, but I guess when faced with the abortion question, when it hit your family, God wasn't big enough to solve that problem, huh? May God forgive you, Sarah. "

Kayla grabbed her purse and silently walked out of the kitchen back door feeling a great sense of loss. She knew that for all of her aunt's faults, Auntie Sarah was completely loyal to her family and would bail them out with money or promises of money in order to fulfill her own goals. In a sense, more than half of her kinfolk in Texas were in Auntie Sarah's pocket for one reason or another. Kayla felt a sense of shame as she turned on the ignition to her white pearl Chrysler 300, a present given to her by Aunt Sarah upon completing her first two crucial college years at Southern Methodist University and drove away in tears.

Sister Pepperdine picked up the dishes left on the table and silently placed them in the sink. As she looked out the window, she thought about all the times she had prayed to bear a child and the many times she had confided to Sarah about her frustrations about being unable to bear a child. With her back turned to Sister Finley she said, "Sarah, you knew how badly I wanted a child. I could have raised Monique's baby." She turned around to see her friend Sarah with both elbows on the table and her head in her hands. "But I know that Monique's baby would have been a constant reminder to you of your family's shame and your lack of control over the situation. You know, you think you truly know a person and then they do something that knocks you off your feet. For years I looked up to you as a person who loved God and would do anything to protect the Kingdom of Christian believers. I've seen you up at the crack of dawn cleaning the church, visiting the sick, helping members with their bills. You would do anything you could to make sure that New Light had a good name in the community. Now, I know you truly could not get over that Pastor Stewart did not make your husband the chairman of the deacon board like he promised under the table during one of your meetings," continued Sister Pepperdine as she walked over to the table.

"I know you didn't know that I knew that piece of information did you? I guess you thought that since my brother Jenkins had lost his wife, he would be too grieved to lead the church. But I prayed for you and I forgave you, and God looked after my brother and gave him strength. I love you, Sarah. We have been friends for more than 50 years, but I was wrong not to let you know when you were doing wrong. I haven't been a good friend to you because I felt I couldn't stop you anyway, so I let you go on and do your damage. I didn't even try to minister to you because I wanted to stay in your good graces. I have seen you talk about people like garbage, and then try to get those same folks to do your dirty work," continued Sister Pepperdine as she grabbed her pocketbook and sunglasses from the table.

"But today, you have been exposed. Your true heart, motives and deeds have been revealed to your best friend and to your favorite niece." Putting her sunshades on, Sister Pepperdine made her way to the back door and on her way out she looked back at her friend and said, "I have a hair appointment today at Heavenly Hands so I will try to check on you later. I pray that *you* pray for forgiveness and I know the good Lord will help you."

Sister Finley began to shake and tremble in tears as she sat at the table. Yet, her heart remained unchanged as she tried to think of a way to smooth this thing over with Kayla and Betty Jean so that her plans for the big pastoral appreciation week would be complete. Her tears flowed only because she had discovered her own weaknesses and began to question her own motivations why she went to church in the first place.

Chapter 19

A New Day

I awoke in my husband's arms and gently kissed him on the lips.

"Good morning sleepy head," I said.

"Good morning, Goldie," Lance said with a look that said, "I want you." So I encouraged him to pass through my Golden Gates.

An hour later, we both showered and had a quiet breakfast together while the kids were still asleep. I decided that I wouldn't say a word about yesterday and what happened, but I would wait until he was ready to talk. I informed Lance that my grandmother Bigmama Thompson and my mother would be in town on Friday for the Pastoral & Family appreciation celebration and that I had a housekeeper scheduled to come in to clean the parsonage real good on Thursday. I reminded him that we had a barbeque planned on Saturday at the community park center for all of our guests and family that would be in town this weekend to help us celebrate our first year at New Light. Lance's family would be in on Thursday and they would be staying at the local Hilton Hotel in Southlake. Most of my family was coming into town on Friday and for many of them this would be their first time setting foot at the New Light Church. We both scheduled our palm pilots for all of this week's personal and church events.

"After this appreciation service, I am going to take at least two Sundays off and you and the kids and I are going to have some family time together. I know this past year has been quite busy for all of us and we haven't had any time to really travel or vacation anywhere. I talked to Deacon Jenkins last night and he agreed that I needed some time away with my family. Would you like to go down to Galveston for one of those weekends?" Lance asked.

"Sure, honey that would be great!" I said as I entered those promised weekend dates in my palm pilot. "I just hope that nobody dies or anything and we would be forced to change our plans. It just seems like every time we plan something to do as a family, the church comes calling for us to rearrange everything. Somebody dies or somebody's second cousin dies and the family requests that you preach, or somebody is deathly ill. It always seems to be something. Remember how we saved all that money to take the kids to Disney World four years ago for a two week vacation and on the way on the road, we got word that one of your deacons died at that church and we had to turn around and drive back home? The kids were so upset and they seemed to cry all the way back home. We still haven't taken them to Disney World. It is just so hard to get excited about anything because there have been so many disappointments in the past," I said lowering my eyes to the table.

"I know, baby. You all have been so supportive of me and my ministry." Lance said walking over to me and planting a kiss on my forehead. "I will make it up to you and the kids. I promise. We are going to take that trip to Disney World next year, no matter what. I think I need to spend some quality time with just Junior and I. That boy is

14 years old and time is going so fast. I am going to try to take him fishing or something and bond with him."

"Fishing? Lance, do you even know how to fish?" I said with a smile on my face.

"Nope, but Deacon Jenkins said that he is going to show me so that I can show Junior," Lance said.

"That is great, sweetheart. I am sure that Junior would enjoy that. I'm going into work early today. Can you make sure that the girls brush their hair? I put a wrap on their hair last night so they should be set to go. Their clothes are ironed in their closet and they know what shoes to wear to school. Make sure that Junior doesn't try to wear his pants sagging to the floor to school today. Connie and Jaylyn have dance practice right after school at 4pm. Can you please have them there on time? And make sure that they all complete their chores and finish their homework before they even think about turning on a TV, playing a video game or talking on the phone. If you need me, just call me at work or on my cell phone. Don't forget to make sure that our bills are paid for this week on the parsonage," I said as I gathered my materials together to take to Victorious Workers.

"Yes, honey. It's Monday and it's my day off but it sure seems like I still have a 24/7 job here at the house. I'll make sure the kids look nice and don't I always ensure that they get to their practices and clean up their room?" Lance said with a hint of sarcasm.

"Yes, right, Lance. I love you, have a good day," I said as I left out of the back door.

I got into our Navigator, put my hands on the stirring wheel and calmly exhaled. "Thank you, Lord." I said to myself. "Thank you for helping me hold my tongue, make passionate love to my man, and keep peace in my home. Now, Lord, I need you to work on him to communicate to me in his own time. Give me patience, in Jesus name, Amen."

I drove to work to Victorious Workers and arrived about 7:00am. The office was quiet. I put on some coffee and checked my messages from Friday when I was off. Our voice mail stated that I had three messages. Two of the messages were from potential workers who wanted to fill out an application. Another message was from Deacon Sable who called on Sunday around 7pm and said that he needed to speak to me immediately upon my return to the office. Deacon Sable was a member of the board of Victorious Workers and a respected deacon of New Light. He was in charge of employee concerns and ethics. Deacon Sable was known for having a bad understanding. It would take a person telling him something three or four times before he received a proper understanding of the issue. However, he was a good man, just a little mentally slow. He was a faithful member and deacon to New Light and a distant cousin of Deacon Finley. I wrote a note to myself to call Deacon Sable after 9:00am today. My assistant, Julie Jones arrived at 7:30am. The one thing I loved about Julie was that she was always 30 minutes early to work every day. She called it her cool time and preparation time to get ready for the day. We had over ten potential workers coming in for interviews this morning and five people being assigned for temporary work. In the last two months, Victorious Workers had successfully placed at least six people into permanent jobs from their temporary assignments. Every Thursday, we held seminars that helped workers learn how to dress for success and how to talk professionally on interviews. We advised them on filling out job applications and providing day care information for families. Our reputation as a reputable temporary agency was quickly growing in Southlake. I had two meetings with area commissioners slated for Tuesday and a luncheon with the Southlake Chamber of Commerce. I worked between 25 to 35 hours a week at Victorious Workers, however I was only paid for twenty hours of work a week because we were still waiting to hear if we were awarded for our second funding grant. We would know within the next two weeks.

I hope that perhaps Deacon Sable was calling with the news that we had received additional funding that would support me working thirty hours at least a week and Julie working full time. She desperately needed more hours. Lance didn't like me to work more than twenty hours a week, but we were trying to save money to send our children to college and perhaps buy our own home so I felt it was necessary for me to help bring in some more income.

I was so nervous that if anything happened to Lance that I would be out in the cold. I had known many pastors' wives that when their husbands died, their churches refused to bury their husbands, or gave them tacky funerals and absolutely refused to help out the widow. Upon coming to New Light, part of Lance's package was a life, health, and funeral insurance policy for him and his family, and within ten years, closing costs to help purchase our own home. At the other churches that Lance pastored, he didn't have any type of benefit package. Once our children were on Medicaid while Lance attended seminary. I used to have nightmares that Lance would die in a car wreck and I would be flat broke with no money to bury him. We put our whole lives into the church and trusted church folks to take care of us. Yet, God gives you common sense as well. Just two years ago, one of Lance's close preacher friends, Reverend Chad Morris died at the age of 36 of an apparent heart attack. His widow was left financially with nothing and her husband's church abandoned her and her five kids. Several local politicians, Lance and a few other pastors went in together to help cover the funeral expenses for this young preacher. Two weeks after burying her husband, the church forced Sister Morris and her children to move out of the church parsonage. Today, she lives in one of the Dallas public housing properties with her five young children. Reverend Morris was not financially prepared to die and he entrusted his family's care to the church where he pastored full-time for over eight years. He had not bothered to invest in any health or life insurance for his family. When Reverend Morris died, he left his family financially insecure.

Lance promised that would not happen to his family and he made the necessary requests to the deacon board at his last church and when they refused to honor his requests for benefits, he prayed and the Lord moved us to New Light with a full health and life benefit package for the entire family. I inhaled as I thought about those years where God's divine providence took care of us and finally God granted my husband wisdom to take care of his family. The ringing of the phone interrupted my memories…

"Good Morning, Victorious Workers. How can I help you?" Julie said. "Good morning Deacon Sable, yes, Mrs. Stevens is here today. I'll put you through to her."

"Good morning Deacon Sable," I said. "What can I do for you?"

"Hello, Sister Stevens. I would like to talk to you in person rather than over the phone. Can I meet you at about 9:00am this morning?" Deacon Sable asked.

"I do have an appointment at 9:00 this morning, but perhaps I can fit you in at 9:30. Is that okay?"

"Sure, that will be fine. I will see you at 9:30."

He hung up and I wondered what he wanted to talk to me about? I advised Julie about my new appointment and asked her to have some coffee and donuts ready for him when he arrived. I cleaned up the office and prepared for my first client.

At 9:25am, Deacon Sable walked in the door looking quite pensive. I walked to the front office and politely greeted him. Victorious Workers was a small edifice with three offices, one bathroom and a break room. I walked Deacon Sable back to my office, which had a side picturesque view of the adjacent Southlake Mall. A picture of Lance, the children and me was on my desk, along with my name-plate. My college degree from the University of Texas hung on my left wall, my online seminary degree in church administration from College of Biblical Studies, my certificate for interior design and my MBA from the University of Phoenix degree hung on the right wall. A picture of our Victorious Workers logo that displayed a man and woman with outstretched arms hung behind my ma-hogany desk. I motioned for Deacon Sable to have a seat. I walked behind my desk and calmly sat down.

Deacon Sable began speaking first.

"Sister Stevens this is quite awkward for me but I must talk to you about this. Who did you notify concerning closing Victorious Work-ers early on Friday? I sent my cousin down here to apply for a job last Friday and no one was here to take his application," he said.

"Now if this office is going to be closed, it is proper protocol to let the board members know, don't you think so?" he said.

"I did inform Deacon Jenkins that I would be out of the office and that Julie was leaving at 12pm," I said.

"When did you let him know and did you ask him? I recall that employees are supposed to request a day off, not inform that they are just taking off," Deacon Sable said with his arm folded against his chest.

"I requested the day off on last Monday, and Deacon Jenkins, who is the President of this board, said that it would be okay. He also knew that Julie would be here until 12pm," I said.

"I thought that you are supposed to contact all of the board members when you are going to be out?" said Deacon Sable.

"Our policy states that I am supposed to notify the chairman of our board. And I did that Deacon Sable," I politely said.

"How is this Julie Jones working out for you? Some of the members of New Light have reported that she is always on the phone making personal phone calls. By the way, did you ever interview Kayla?" Deacon Sable asked.

"First of all, we do receive a lot of calls from persons looking for employment and I haven't noticed that Ms. Jones is making any personal phone calls but I will look into that matter and no, I didn't get a chance to interview with Kayla because I had already hired Ms. Jones."

I stood up from my desk. "Can I get you some more coffee?" I asked.

"No, sister, that is okay. I was just concerned that this office was closed and I didn't know why. At any rate, how are you doing after what happened yesterday at the church?" asked Deacon Sable.

I shifted nervously from one leg to another. "What happened yesterday at church, Deacon?"

"Well, you know, with uh, Sister Marilyn Steele calling the pastor by his first name. We found out he appointed her temporary financial secretary and he did not receive a quorum from the deacon board to approve it. And your husband bought all that new furniture in his office and didn't get approval to purchase those materials with church funds. There are a lot of things happening within our church and its happening too fast if you ask me. So, when I found out that this here office was closed Friday and I didn't know about it, I decided to investigate. Sarah, told me that she stopped by and saw this office closed and then she told me to look in the pastor's office to see his new furniture and for the life of me I couldn't understand how our pastor could afford such expensive furniture and,"

I interjected, "Sarah, uh, Sister Sarah Finley stopped by on Friday?"

"Yes, maam, she called me early Sunday morning, about 5:30am, and told me because she felt that it was proper that all the board persons be notified when a church business is closed on a normal business day and that she didn't think it was right for the pastor to purchase items in excess of $5,000 without deacon approval. She has been pushing for us to put Pastor on a worker's contract since he first came to New Light. Well, if he continues to break policy we need to at least suspend him. I know Sister Finley has been hot at me because I am against putting a preacher on a contract. If this is true, maybe we should put Pastor on a contract after all," said Deacon Sable as he looked at the floor.

I sat down at my desk and my spirit began to discern that there was something evil at work and Deacon Sable was being used in the game.

"If you don't mind me asking Sister Stevens, but is everything okay at the house? Are you and Pastor getting along? Some of the members are beginning to talk about how Sister Steele is always in Pastor's face all the time. Pastor has really started to place her in some powerful leadership positions and she has only been at New Light for six months."

Okay, by this time I was getting a little angry that this man was trying to talk about my husband and insinuate that my husband was not being faithful. In essence, he was disrespecting both my husband and me. I hate it when church members try to pry into our personal lives. Furthermore, it was improper for him to discuss my husband's employment with me or anyone else that was not on the deacon board. I said a silent prayer for the Lord to help me keep my cool.

"Deacon Sable, Pastor and I are fine. I know you know that Pastor is great at helping members to find their place within the church. Sister Steele is an old friend of Pastor and I can assure you that they are only friends. Let's not let the rumor mill of New Light get the best of us," I said as I walked around my desk motioning toward the door.

"We have a great church and a great pastor. You must excuse me Deacon Sable, but I do have a 9:45 appointment, but if you have any concerns about office closures, please be sure to check with Deacon Jenkins. I am very good about following Victorious Workers personnel policies and protocol," I said.

Deacon Sable stood up from his chair and began to walk out of the door. "Thanks for straightening that out for me. Your office really looks nice and I am glad to hear that you and Pastor are doing fine. Now maybe, Sarah Finley will leave me alone with all her concerns. You know how demanding she can be. I don't know how Abraham Finley has put up with her for all these years," he said.

I looked at him and smiled without saying a word. I have learned that sometimes it is better to be silent and besides I didn't want him to carry anything I said inappropriately back to Sister Finley. "You have a good day, Deacon," I said.

I walked him to the front door and said goodbye. My 9:45 am appointment was seated waiting for me to conduct his interview. I went into the bathroom and checked myself over. A small quick tear fell from my eye. It had secretly escaped. I exhaled, cleared the black trail of mascara that the watery tear had formed and returned to my duties as supervisor of Victorious Workers Temporary Agency.

Chapter 20

A Wonderful and Meaningful Experience

I was looking forward to my family coming in to town on this Friday for the appreciation service. It was one of the few things that I liked about the appreciation service celebrations. Our family would all come down to encourage us and spend some time with us. We also scheduled fun activities for the children on that Saturday. Lance had ordered a moonwalk for the children to jump in and the brotherhood of New Light volunteered to provide the barbeque. I sat at my desk after a long day and looked over my palm pilot for my schedule. Connie and Jaylyn and I had a hair appointment on Thursday and I was going to pick up my dress with matching hat, shoes and accessories that I had ordered out of a catalog at one of the boutiques in Southlake on Friday. I didn't want to wear anything that any of the women in Southlake had been seen in so I special ordered my dress for the appreciation service. Lance had taken Junior about a month ago to purchase a new suit with matching Stacy Adams shoes. I prayed that he could still fit those clothes. He was growing like a weed. My mother purchased Connie and Jaylyn's dresses, matching bows and shoes for Sunday and she was bringing them with her. Lance decided to just have an 11:00am appreciation service because a lot of the members could not find time to attend any of the 3:30pm afternoon services.

After his first three months at New Light, Lance began to cut back on afternoon services and completely eliminated the 6pm Sunday evening service for lack of support. This angered Sister Finley because it was a New Light tradition to have an evening service. She let it be known that she was very upset about this change and surveyed the deacon board with the question "How would New Light survive without the offerings and the occasional chicken sale dinners held at the evening services?" Lance called her in for a meeting to dispel her ramblings and told her that the Bible encouraged that the church be maintained through tithes and offerings. I think Sister Finley was upset because Lance put a stop to her mission group's annual chicken dinner sale that often netted her group over $500 per sale event. "These folks are not going to give money up for free and Pastor Stevens you will see that for yourself."

Instead, the tithers in New Light, grew from 25% to a whopping 42% within the church because Lance put a stop to weekly and monthly dues within ministries, bake sales and chicken sales. The only ministry that was allowed to raise funds outside of the evangelistic CD, video and audio ministry, was the Youth ministry, and that was limited to car washes, T-shirt sales and donations. Most of the children did not work so Lance compromised on events that warranted more money for the children to be exposed to other things outside of Southlake.

I closed the office at 5:30pm and proceeded to go home. I knew that Lance would have the children's dinner on. I went to pick up Connie and Jaylyn from dance practice. I was exhausted from a mentally draining day and I was having a hard time focusing on my work. I did receive some good news that another one of our temporary workers that we had placed at a local law firm had been asked to stay on permanently. I loved my job and I loved hearing good news especially on days when I needed to hear it.

I picked up the girls from dance practice and drove home. They talked to me all the way about school and dance practice. They were so excited that Bigmama Thompson and Granny Eva would be coming into town and they couldn't wait to see their new dresses. I drove into our driveway and I was alarmed to find the house eerily dark. I walked into the kitchen and turned on the light switch but there was no light. Connie tried to turn on the TV, but there was not any power.

"Mommy," she said, "the TV won't come on and where are all the lights?"

Our lights were out. Memories of past experiences in church parsonages where someone forgot to pay the bill or Lance forgot to give it to the finance team began to numb my brain. A feeling of familiar fear ran up my spine sending a small chill. I told the girls to get back in the car and we would eat out tonight. Why didn't Lance call me on my cell phone to let me know? I would have never come home with the girls if the lights were out. I hated trying to explain to them what was going on. When they were smaller, I used to tell them that we were having dinner by candlelight and that it was a special night for mothers and their children. Lance would be out trying to find the nearest deacon or the person who forgot to pay the bill. I was slightly confused. New Light was doing very well financially and it didn't make sense for the parsonage lights to be turned off.

I backed the car out of the driveway and we made our way to the nearest McDonald's. I called Lance's cell phone number and I noticed that he tried to call me at least three times but I guess I turned my ringer off by mistake. I wondered why he didn't try to call me at work. I dialed Lance's office phone.

"Hello?" Lance answered on the second ring.

"Hey, babe, the lights are not working at the house. What is going on?" I asked trying to remain calm.

"I am not sure but I am at the church and I am trying to contact the light company's after hours number to see if someone can come out and restore our lights. If they won't come out, then I will call the mayor of Southlake if I have to. I am trying to find out how this happened, but no one on the deacon board is taking responsibility and I can't locate Marilyn anywhere. Somebody dropped the ball and I will get to the bottom of it."

"Have you and Junior eaten yet? I am taking the girls to McDonald's for dinner. Is Junior with you?" I asked.

"Yes, I picked him up from school and we were both at home when the lights went out and no, I don't have much of an appetite right now. I took Junior by Jack-N-the-Box to grab a burger. Look, I'm sorry baby. I'll get to the bottom of this," Lance said.

"Okay, we should be at the church after we eat. I love you, Lance," I said.

"I love you, too. Goldie."

Later on that night, the electrician came out to our home and restored power by 10:30pm. While we were out, the gas company had come and disconnected the gas and our land phone was permanently disconnected. It was if someone had purposefully called all our utility companies and told them we were moving or something.

Lance was tired and confused. We dressed for bed and he held me in his arms.

"I promised you that you wouldn't have to ever deal with this sort of stuff again. And here we are with no gas, no phone and for the life of me I don't know what I did or why this has happened. Deacon Jenkins assured me that he would investigate," Lance said.

"Its okay, sweetie. As long as I have you and the kids and we are together and healthy that is all that really matters right now," I said. I thank God that He is my strength because I remember a time I might have called all of those deacons and given them a piece of my mind because all of our major utilities were turned off.

"I promised your daddy that I would take care of you. Sometimes, you know I doubt my ministry and I just want to throw in the towel. I know I could do right by my family if I worked in Corporate America and made big bucks. Yet, the Lord won't allow me to quit this preaching business. I'm like Jeremiah, "God's Word is like fire, shut up in my bones!" said Lance in his preaching voice. He held me tighter. "So, are you are going to be okay when you have to take a cold shower tomorrow morning?" he asked

"I don't want to think about that right now. We'll deal with that in the morning. I am glad that the phones are not ringing off the hook though. Remind me that if our gas is not on by the morning I need to go and purchase the Morris family a cake for their son who was injured. Is he still in the hospital?" I asked Lance

"Yeah, baby, their son is still in the hospital. What would I do without you? Here we are with no phone or gas service and you are still sweet enough to remember that I asked you to bake a cake for the Morris family. If you are too tired don't worry about it," Lance said.

"No, I don't want to let that family down. It won't be a problem, Lance. I know how I would feel if Junior was in the hospital right now. I may not have a phone or gas right now, but I do have my family all together and that is a blessing. I just hope we get this thing situated before our family gets in town. That would sure be very embarrassing. They are looking forward to coming to meet our new church family" I said.

"Did you all ever catch up with Sister Marilyn?" I asked trying to see if Lance was ready to talk about the situation that happened at church. I stroked his arm as my head lay within his bosom.

"Not yet. Deacon Jenkins said that her phone number has been changed and the new one is unlisted now. She wasn't at her office and her boss said that she took a leave of absence for three weeks," Lance said.

"Sunday, I was so embarrassed by what she said about me. She caught me totally by surprise with her hug and quick kiss. I think she was the one who personally bought me all of that new furniture in my office. I am still not sure who had access to my office. I knew that Deacon Finley was creating new key locks but he never informed me when he was going to do it until he contacted me in Austin while preaching out of town. He apparently gave Marilyn a key to my office. I let him know that I wanted my office re-keyed next week and only certain people would have access to my pastor's study. I told him that I didn't want any of my female staff to have my office key because of the potential turmoil it could cause. He agreed with me wholeheartedly. You know, I have known Marilyn since she was eight years old. Her family is from Houston and she would come there every summer to visit her grandparents. We weren't particularly close growing up because I was six years older than her. I ran into her at a Florida Christian convention and she told me that she would be relocating to Texas and that she would look me up when she returned to live here," Lance said stroking my hair, ever so gently.

"When she showed up in Southlake and joined New Light just two months after seeing her in Florida. I was shocked and very un-comfortable with her presence. I knew that she had been baptized before because I saw my Uncle Rupert baptize her when she was ten-years-old at our home church in Houston but she told me that she wanted *me* to baptize her. She then showed me a picture of her new fiancé who was back in Florida. She said he was going to move to Texas within the year. I thought perhaps that I had judged her wrong. She always talked about her wedding plans and how she was going to get married. She was planning for her wedding to be two times as spiritual as Juanita Bynum's wedding. Somehow, I think that young lady is not even planning to get married. Sister Finley suggested that we appoint her as the new temporary admin-istrative assistant and allow her to lead the Women's Ministry at the church. I informed Sister Finley that Marilyn had a full time job and would not be able to keep any church hours. And then the very next day, Marilyn shows up to work in the secretary's office," Lance said. "It was rather strange."

I sat up and looked into his eyes, "You know I love you, and I trust you. But whatever you decide to do to expose this woman make sure you have a witness, because she can turn this thing around on you. I know most preachers may go through a circumstance where their character and integrity will be scrutinized," I said. "But I must tell you, my female radar tells me that something is not right with this woman and my spirit tells me that Sister Finley may have set this whole thing up. Sister Finley's name just comes up too often when there are negative issues within the church," I said.

I wondered if I should tell him about Deacon Sable's visit to my office today and what he tried to insinuate about Lance and Marilyn. I decided to wait to share that information, as the day had already been a trying one for him.

"Let's get some rest, sweetheart. Don't forget to get on your knees and say your prayers," I said.

"I can say my prayers lying in this bed," he said.

"Come on Lance, let's get on our knees," I said as I knelt beside our bed. "This is a position of worship and humbleness. Now, if the Muslims can get on their knees five times a day and pray toward Mecca to Muhammad, I know we can get on our knees at least once a day and pray to the Almighty God," I coaxed Lance.

He rolled over and knelt on the floor beside me. I realized that it had been at least a year since Lance and I had prayed together on our knees in private. He looked at me and said, "Okay, you pray." Even though my husband was the great preacher pastor in public, I often found that I was the spiritual prayer warrior at home. I closed my eyes and began to talk out loud to God in prayer:

185

"Lord, Jesus. How we love Thy name. For you are holy, holy, holy, worthy is the Lamb of God. You are awesome and your wonders are marvelous to behold. Thank you, Lord for your daily mercies. Tonight, God we confess our sins to you and we pray for your forgiveness. We decree your blessings, oh Lord, in the lives of our family. We stand in faith and bind every enemy that has been set in place to hinder and thwart the purposes that you have for our lives. We pray in the name of Jesus that our spiritual enemies are exposed and that their works be uprooted and destroyed this very moment.... We pray in Jesus name that angels be released to defend the well- being of our family, the well- being of God's Kingdom in our lives together...that the principalities at work in our lives be devoured by the swords of the angels of the Lord.

We pray the enemy be confused and confounded, and that they be entangled in the plans, traps, and snares that they have set for us. We decree peace! We decree, Oh God, your perfect order in our lives! We decree that your plan and purposes be fulfilled this day at this very moment.

We bind the ruling forces over our church, New Light... the forces seated in the highest ruling places... that their plans come to ruin... in Jesus name...

And it is in Jesus' name that we decree ...that nothing that you have in store for us be held up in the realm of the spirit....that everything You, oh Lord, desire for us during this season....it shall be...that it is so... that it be released unto us and our family... None of God's favor from us shall be withheld...none of God's finances from us shall be with held, none of God's miracles from us shall be withheld...in Jesus name...

And finally, we pray ...we decree that we are able to rightly discern the times and seasons and to pray accordingly.

In Jesus name, we lift up this prayer to you, Oh God! Let your will be done in our lives, Amen.

I looked over at Lance and he was silently crying. I reached over to him and grabbed him and held my husband in my arms and we wept together. I knew that my husband was probably enduring more than he cared to share with me. I understood that there are some things that men had to bear alone with just Jesus. I am learning not to always pick him with questions, but just be there for him to lean on and provide emotional support. I wondered if Deacon Sable had stopped by the house or called him today as well. I knew that though our journey through the years had been tough, we had learned to make it together with Jesus. This journey was a wonderful and meaningful experience because it taught us to trust in God and lean not unto our own understanding. We both understood that we don't fight against people but we fight against our great adversary, Satan, who tries to use every trick in his book to keep us from our God given purpose.

Lance and I returned underneath our bedcovers. He grabbed his bible and began silently reading Hebrews 6:10, a scripture that Lance would read and reread when he needed encouragement. It reads as such: *God is not unjust; he will not forget your work and the love you have shown him as you have helped his people and continue to help them.*

I watched his lips move as he spoke the scripture silently and meditated on its promise.

I picked up my journal and wrote:

Dear First Lady,

Well, it seems to be happening again that our lights were turned off, the gas and the phone service all in one day. I prayed that New Light would be different from the other churches Lance pastored but I guess all churches are alike in some ways. It seems that some-one dropped the ball on paying the parsonage bills and I guess that someone must be upset with the Lance about something. I know that Lance has something on his mind but he is not really talk-ing about it right now. He did let me know that he knew Marilyn Steele casually from Houston, TX, but he still did not share why he didn't communicate that to me when she joined New Light. But, First Lady, you would have been proud of me. I kept my cool and held my tongue to a limit and didn't go off and I even prayed for him without starting an argument about who would pray. I am growing. God is giving me new strength everyday. I am still praying that he removes some of my evil thoughts that I have toward Sister Finley. I know if I don't deal with this anger, I might actually go off and hit that old sister. But I must remember that in the words of my mother and I quote, "this life was meant to be a wonderful and meaningful experience." Though situations in my life have served as the thorn in my flesh. I know that my thorns shape me for better service in God's army.

This is Lance's first appreciation service celebration week at New Light. Our relatives will be in town soon and I am praying that everything will be nice this weekend. I am now looking forward to this celebration to see what God is going to do. The kids and I have a surprise to give to Lance on his big day. I can't wait until he sees it! He is really going to like it! Well, good night, First Lady, I will talk to you soon.

Love,

Jackie

Chapter 21

A Family Reunion

At 12pm sharp, my Bigmama Thompson and my mother Eva Montgomery turned their big Escalade Cadillac SUV into my drive way. It had been 11 months since I had traveled to Richmond to see my family so I was eager to see them. My two sisters were planning on coming to town on Saturday. I ran out of the front door to greet them. A tall, lean man with a black Kango hat opened the front door and proceeded to open the rear back seat car door.

"For you my lady," I heard him say. My mother got out of the backseat and carefully placed her perfectly French manicured toenails on the concrete. "Thank you, Mr. Bentley. Can you please hand me my white sandals? Where will you be staying for the weekend?" she quizzed.

"I will be at the local Hilton Hotel if you all need me. I'll get your luggage and place it in the house," Mr. Bentley retrieved their luggage from the car and placed it within the parsonage. "Hi, baby" my mother said to me with outstretched arms. She gave me her trademark kiss on both cheeks. "Ooh, your house is lovely." I knew it could never compare with her mini mansion back at home. But this was the best parsonage Lance and I had ever lived in since he began pastoring. My Bigmama Thompson creaked her way out of the Cadillac and strolled over to me with her new walker ensemble.

"Bigmama, when did you start walking on a walker?" I questioned. "Nobody told me that you were walking on a walker now!"

"Well, if you weren't so busy with your husband's church and all, you would know that I started walking on a walker about two months ago," Bigmama said.

"Gul', you know I am just playin' with you," she said in her classic Texas country drawl. "This here is Mr. Woods' old walker, he is just letting me use it just in case I need it if we get a ticket, cuz' you know how those laws like to stop us colored folk on the road. So, I told Bentley that if any of those cops stopped us to tell them that I had a mini stroke, so that we could get a warning or something," Bigmama said as she reared back and laughed her customary contagious laugh that caused her entire body to shake. "Gul', get over here and give your Bigmama Thompson a hug."

I walked over to my Bigmama and gave her the tightest hug and kiss on her cheek. At 83, my Bigmama Thompson was still a wise cracker and could still wear a pair of 3-inch heels any day. My mother developed her since of style and got her lean, long legs from my Bigmama. I instantly thought that Sister Peterson and Bigmama T would probably hit it off great this weekend. I only hoped that Sister Peterson wouldn't try to spread her poison to Bigmama T about what is going on in our church.

I walked them into the parsonage and I was so glad that the maid service had sent extra help to clean the house. My house was sparkling clean and it smelled absolutely divine. I seated them both in the living room.

"Now where are those grandbabies of mine? I can't wait to see them," my mother said.

"The kids are still at school," I said.

"Where is that fine, hunk of a preachaman that you married? Where is my grandson-in-law, Lance?" Bigmama asked.

"He is at the church right now, but he is coming home for lunch. He should be here any minute," I said.

I was grateful to God that my lights were on, the gas was back on and the phone service was reconnected. The housecleaner had come and done a superb job with the house. The girls and I had gone to the beauty salon and we received a gorgeous spiral roller set from Ms. Vivian, who in turn let me know that she had notified Lance that she was willing to give a solo on our appreciation day. I was looking forward to hearing her sing. Upon hearing the news that she would be singing and playing the organ on Sunday, several of her customers within the salon remarked that they would be in attendance to hear Vivian Daniels return to the church and sing again.

I gave my mama and Bigmama a tour of the parsonage. They both loved the prayer nook and remarked how New Light must really care for their pastoral family. I didn't let them know that Lance and I had personally paid for the upgrades within the house. "Now, baby," my mother began, "when are you and Lance going to finally purchase your own home? Because you know when that man closes his eyes in death, those church folks are going to want you out of their property, so you make sure that you and Lance make plans for that. Mama, didn't raise no fool and I didn't send you to college so that you could land flat on your behind," she said as she smoothed out her ivory linen Capri pantsuit.

"I know Mama. We are working on that as we speak," I said.

"Good!" she exclaimed giving me another hug. "This is the best looking parsonage you and Lance have ever lived in."

"Okay, Eva Montgomery, stop being so judgmental and let's go to our room to unpack. Jackie, you know your Bigmama had to go through Elgin and get my baby some sausage. I got it in my luggage just for you," Bigmama Thompson said.

"Oh, Bigmama, I am staying away from pork right now. It's only chicken and fish for me now. I am trying to lose these 15 pounds I gained since we have moved to Southlake," I said.

"Yeah, I did notice that you have picked up some weight," my mother said as she inspected me from top to bottom. "You know that you are an emotional eater. Is everything all right? The last time you picked up a lot of weight was when you and Lance were at that God forsaken church in the country, what was the name of that church? Bethel or Little Zion? I thought those folks were going to cause my baby to have a nervous breakdown. You gained over 20 pounds in six months," my mother said as she held me tight.

"Mama, I am doing fine and we are blessed to be at New Light. I haven't been jogging as much as I used to. I have lost eight pounds within the last three weeks, though. So I know the weight will fall off," I said, shifting nervously from one foot to the other.

"Well, who's going to eat all this sausage?" Bigmama T asked.

"Bigmama, you got a 14-year-old great-grandson who can eat all of that pork in one sitting. So, don't worry about it, your food will not go to waste," I said reaching out to grab her within our sister to sister circle hug. "I miss you all so much. Why can't Richmond be right around the corner?" I playfully asked.

Just then Lance entered the back door. "Will you look at this, yawl are already cuddled up next to each other. Hello, Mama Eva and Bigmama T! It is so good to see you!" Lance said, as he gave them each a hug.

"My, my," my mother said, "don't you look prosperous and very handsome? You must have found a good church this time. You look great, Lance! Are you taking good care of my Jackie like her daddy told you to? Because you know I think that man will rise up from the grave if any man abused any of his daughters," Mama said, sarcastically with a smile on her face.

"Yes, maam, I am. And I am trying my best to spoil her," Lance said giving me a peck on the cheek.

"Yawl are so cute together," Bigmama T said. "Now after we eat, I want to see your office place Jackie. What is it called again?"

"Victorious Workers," I said.

"I still can't believe those chu'ch folks even allowed the preacha's wife to run their business. Now I know that times are a changin'. In my day, they were to sit pretty, wear those tall chu'ch hats and they bet not dare say a word in the Lawd's house. Today, preacha's wives are helpin' to run the chu'ch businesses and even obtaining seminary degrees too. What you say!! I know the Lawd is on his way back to get His chuch'!" Bigmama T said.

We all laughed at her antics. I went into the kitchen and prepared our lunch. We all sat down and ate together. I noticed that Lance seemed to have a "forced" smile upon his face during our lunch. Afterward as we prepared to drive mama and Bigmama T over to the Victorious Workers office, I cornered Lance and asked, "Sweetie, is everything okay? You look a little pensive," I said, as I gently placed my hand on the side of his face.

"Yes, it's just that Deacon Sable came to visit me this morning in my office and he told me about all of these rumors that are floating around town about me," Lance said.

"What rumors?" I asked

"I am going to need you to come to a Deacon's meeting with me tonight at 7pm at the church," Lance said.

"Why do I have to attend a meeting? You know I don't like going to a witch-hunt session. I've gone through that before. Why can't you speak for me? Aren't you my husband? You promised me Lance that you wouldn't allow another church to gang up on me," I said, as tears began forming in my eyes.

"Baby, wait, just listen," Lance said, as he held my arms on both sides. "They are trying to say that I slept with Marilyn Steele. They are saying that I made a romantic pass at our last musician, Brother Joseph and that's why he quit. And, they are trying to say that you are refusing to notify the Victorious Workers board about your missed days at work. Now we know that this is not true. However, we still have to deal with these allegations and face them."

"What does Deacon Jenkins have to say about all of this?" I asked

"He is very upset about it and believes that Sister Finley is behind all of this; our light, gas and phone being terminated; our secretary quitting last week; my redecorated office, and the mysterious disappearance of Marilyn Steele," Lance said.

"Who brought allegations against you and me?" I asked.

"Deacon Sable came into my office this morning with over 50 signatures of New Light parishioners who have requested a formal review of me, due to these rumors," Lance said looking at the floor.

"Can they do that?" I asked

"We are not sure yet. Deacon Jenkins is at our attorney's office right now going over our church bylaws, procedures and policies. I have asked our area bishop to come to the meeting tonight to mediate," Lance said.

"Oh, Lance, I am so sorry," I said, as I put my arms around his neck and hugged him tight. "I'm so sorry. You know I love you and I will stand with you tonight. I'll tell mama and Bigmama T that something came up and I'll ask Sister Peterson to come over and keep them company while we are out," I said, giving him a kiss on both his cheeks.

"I am going to stand in the Lord. I know that this is a process where God will weed out and reveal my enemies. Thank you for your prayer the other night. It really strengthened me," Lance said. "You have always stood by me through it all. You have a way of smiling through all of our tests and trials. I know you are my gift from God. None of these rumors are true. I have been faithful to you. I have never compromised our marriage through a physical or emotional affair. I am not perfect, but that is one sin I know I haven't committed in our marriage."

"I know, sweetheart. I know. God has not revealed to me that you have been with anyone outside of our marriage. I will testify to this fact tonight. I can't believe that Brother Joseph is trying to say that you made a romantic pass at him. Everyone knows that he is just ticked off because you fired him. Why would they give credence to a suspect character like him? I just feel like whooping up on Sister Finley, but I know that wouldn't be the Christian thing to do. And I am praying that the thought of revenge flee from my spirit," I said, as my body tightened up at the very thought of Sarah Finley.

"Vengeance is mine, said the Lord. Let's allow Him to work this out for us. I need you at the church by 6:00pm. Deacon Jenkins and I are meeting early for prayer and I want you to join us," said Lance.

"Okay. I will be there. Now, we better get downstairs before those old women downstairs think we are doing something else besides talking," I joked.

We took my mama and Bigmama T to the office building of Victorious Workers. They marveled at the professionalism of the office and the biblical scripture decals posted on each wall. There were information brochures about New Light and its ministries in the front office. Each office was equipped with a Dell Flat Screen Computer and both Julie and I had our own personal Dell laptops in storage for home use. I introduced them to my assistant Julie and told them that she was a member of New Light. I explained to them about our Wall of Fame of temporary workers who had been placed in permanent positions from their temporary assignment. As of today eight Victorious Workers had been placed in permanent positions, their names, picture and new position aligned our Wall of Blessings.

"Baby, I am so proud of you and Lance. This is a wonderful way to bless the kingdom of God. You are instructing and providing a quality workforce," my mama said. "This is what I knew you could do, besides sitting down in church every Sunday in your church hat. I'm glad that your daddy's good money and my networks are beginning to pay off," she said, as she stroked her Della Reese-like hair.

"Yeah. This here is a nice office. Your Bigmama T is proud of you too!" said Bigmama.

My cell phone rang. I answered and it was my college friend, and Lance's cousin, Amanda Deshay on the line.

"Hello?" I said.

"Hey, girl, this is Amanda. I just arrived at the Hilton Hotel. I just wanted you to know that I am in town for you and Lance's big day. His parents should be here some time tonight. Is the big barbeque still planned for tomorrow? Even though I live in Los Angeles, I still miss that good ole' East Texas Barbeque!" she said with a huge laugh. "Has Bigmama T and Mama Eva arrived yet?"

"Yeah, girl, they arrived around noon today. I really miss you and I can't wait to see you."

"Where is that cousin of mine?" Amanda asked.

"Lance? He is at the church. Give him a call. I'm sure he would love to hear your voice right now."

"Hey, I'll do that. But first, I am going to go down to the hot tub downstairs and relax," Amanda said.

I walked around the corner, where my mama and Bigmama T would not be able to hear me.

"Listen, Lance and I have a meeting at 6pm tonight at the church. Do you think you can come over to the parsonage and keep my mama and Bigmama T company?"

"A meeting? Isn't this supposed to be the week that you guys relax? Is everything okay?" she asked.

"Everything is fine. I will share with you about it later," I said.

"Sure, I'll come over to your house about 5:30pm. Girl, you are in my prayers," she said.

"Hey, and don't just say that you are going to pray for me. I need you to intercede for us around 7pm tonight," I requested.

"Sure. I will lift the both of you up in prayer around 7pm, tonight. Done! Now you know if you need me to bring a prayer and a shotgun I will!" She said, with a hearty laugh.

"Girl, you are so crazy. I'll talk to you later on tonight. Good-bye," I said.

I calmly exhaled. I was glad that God had sent my best friend to Texas to help me shoulder this burden. Amanda was an enthusiastic prayer warrior and she was accustomed to interceding for Lance and me over the years. I needed a Barnabas' touch at this moment and Amanda was my Barnabus. She was my shoulder to lean on and cry to; I've never known her to break our confidentiality with one another. She lived in Los Angeles, California, yet her friendship and her love for Lance and I closed the gap on the miles that separated us. In essence, she was Lance's cousin, but she was my one true friend.

Chapter 22

The Meeting

I drove my white pearl Lincoln Navigator into the church parking lot at ten minutes to 6pm. I walked into the church and pulled the olive oil from my purse. I began to walk around the church and anoint the pews, praying at the same time. I anointed the pulpit, the piano, the organ, the deacon pews, and finally I walked into the boardroom where our meeting would be held and I anointed the doors of the room, the table and the seats. I prayed earnestly that God would honor this symbol of faith. I knew that the power was not in the oil but in the power of God. I prayed that His will be done in this meeting. As I finished this prayer, Lance and Deacon Jenkins walked in. I slipped the bottle of oil in my purse and the three of us joined hands in prayer. We each took turns praying for this situation. Deacon Jenkins began to cry as he prayed about the history of New Light and the previous turmoil that took a great man of God away from this church. He interceded for a church that he had invested his entire life in. I knew and understood that Deacon Jenkins loved this church dearly and for the right reasons. His love for his church did not have to do with family loyalty, legacy or obligation; it had to do exclusively with his love of God and His sanctuary of worship.

At 6:55pm, the other eight Deacons of New Light began to show up for the meeting. Deacon Sable showed up at 7:15pm with his notebook of paperwork. Bishop Needly of Greater Praise Church in Dallas, arrived at 7:00pm to serve as mediator. He finally opened the meeting.

"We are gathered here today to discuss the request for a formal review of Pastor Lance McClain Stevens concerning allegations of adultery, homosexuality and misuse of church funds," said Bishop Needly.

My heart sank as I listened to these allegations. I gripped the sides of my chair and held on tight. Lance was seated to my right and Deacon Jenkins on my left. Bishop Needly sat at the head of the table. Five of the deacons sat on the right with Deacon Sable and the other three sat on the other side of Deacon Jenkins. Oddly enough, Deacon Abraham Finley was not present at the meeting. Perhaps he was running late.

"Is there evidence to suggest that these allegations are true?" Bishop Needly asked

"We have 50 signatures from New Light members that have suggested that they too have heard these allegations about Pastor Stevens," said Deacon Sable.

"I need proof. Do you have any evidence, Deacon?" requested Bishop Needly.

"Why, no… I just have these signatures. I do have receipts where over $5,000 of church funds was used to purchase his office furniture," Deacon Sable said.

"Our bylaws state the senior pastor cannot spend more than $500 of church funds within three months, without an approval from the majority of the deacon board," placing the receipts from the various stores in front of the bishop. "And about $5000 is missing from New Light's general fund," Deacon Sable continued.

"How do you respond Pastor Stevens?" the bishop asked.

"I did not authorize any furniture to be purchased. I walked into my office on last Sunday morning and the furniture was there. Someone reorganized my desk and everything. I didn't buy the furniture or the electronic equipment," Lance said, implying that this was a set up.

Deacon Williams spoke up next. "Well, we sure as hell, didn't authorize it Pastor. Did any of the other Deacon's authorize this transaction?"

All of the deacons shook their hands and said, "No."

"Has anyone bothered to ask Deacon Finley for a financial report or ledgers of the transactions?" Lance asked.

"Deacon Finley has been sick with the flu since Tuesday and Sarah won't even let anyone come within ten feet of him. So no, we don't have a record of the last month transactions," Deacon Jenkins said.

"Maybe, your sister Betty Jean can get it for us, since she and Sarah are best friends," Deacon Williams asked.

"No. I don't want to breathe any of this nonsense to any of our members. Therefore, I have not said a word to her about any of this and I suggest to you all that you don't spread this poison and vicious lies to any of your wives," Deacon Jenkins said, as he wagged his fingers at the other deacons around the table.

"You are right, Jenkins," They all agreed.

"Since there is no evidence to support *who* made the purchases, we will move on the other issues of sexual misconduct," said Bishop Needly.

At that moment, I thought I would faint. This is all too much. Lord, give me strength.

"Is there any evidence that proves the allegations of sexual misconduct?" Bishop asked.

Deacon Sable pulled out a torn letter from his jacket pocket. "This was turned in to a deacon last Sunday. It was found in the secretary's office. It is a love note addressed to Pastor Stevens."

"I will attempt to read it so that all persons at this meeting will hear. I need one of you good deacons to make sure that you are taking minutes of this meeting," requested Bishop Needly. He cleared his throat and began to read the words on the crumbled up piece of paper that was torn in two and had been re-taped together.

Dear Pastor Stevens,
Every night I think of you. My heart is full of love for you. I wish that I was your First Lady. I can give you what she cannot. I see how you look at me. I watch your eyes move from my bosom to my ankles.

This could all be yours if only you would make your move. I am here for you. I see the passion in your eyes when you look at me and say, 'Good morning, my sister' on Sunday mornings. You know it just doesn't have to be on Sunday mornings? You could say 'good morning' to me every morning if you'd like. I have a condo in Plano, TX and no one would know that it is our love nest. I have enclosed the condo key for your pleasure. Meet me there this Monday afternoon at 12pm and I will make it worth your while. God has given us this passion for one another and you were meant to be mine. I long for your love. My body groans to become one with you. You know who I am because I hear your body calling out to mine every Sunday morning.
Signed Anonymous Sister

Lance was shifting uncomfortably in his chair. I looked over at him and gently stroked his hand. His face was completely flushed.

Lord, Jesus give me strength and the peace that surpasses all understanding I thought.

"Would you like to respond, Pastor Stevens?" asked Bishop Needly

"This is a letter I received about two weeks ago. It is not uncommon for preachers to get anonymous notes from parishioners. I immediately tore the letter up and threw it away. So, now I know that someone has been snooping around in my office trash can, if the letter is in your hands. I typically just ignore those distractions. This note, however, does not prove that I have been involved in sexual misconduct," Lance said, angrily pounding his hand on the table.

I slunk down a little in my seat. *Another letter? Why didn't he tell me that he received an anonymous letter? I thought to myself and how many letters had he received before?*

"Where is the condo key, Pastor Stevens?" asked Deacon Sable with a sly grin on his face.

"What? I placed that condo key in the trash as well Deacon Sable, or do you have it?" Lance asked looking him straight in the eye.

Deacon Sable turned beet red in the face.

Bishop Needly loudly cleared his throat.

"Do you have any evidence of sexual misconduct, Deacon Sable?" Bishop asked.

"No, this is all I have. The other allegations of a homosexual pass from Pastor to Brother Ray Joseph, the deacons and I believe is completely untrue. We know that Brother Joseph is upset because he was fired. He should have been fired a long time ago," Deacon Sable said, with a defeated look on his face.

I looked at him from across the table and the man could not even look me in the eye.

"There is just one more thing, it is minor, but since we are here, we might as well bring it up," Deacon Sable said. "Mrs. Stevens took two days of work off this week and she took another day off last week and I don't' think that is right or fair. Furthermore, she hired Julie Jones and completely bypassed our member Kayla Clarke, not even for an interview," he continued.

I looked at him like I was Michael the angel and I was going to slay him with my sword. But I remembered my prayer, "Lord, reveal to us our enemies." Even though Lance and I had been there for Deacon Sable when his son died of a cocaine overdose during the first few months of Lance's pastorship at New Light, here he was betraying us and being petty about small issues.

"Wait a minute, Deacon Sable. We are here to talk about the request for a formal review of Pastor Steven's tenure as shepherd over this flock. We are not here to malign his wife. That is a question for the board of Victorious Workers," said Bishop Needly. "Is there anymore evidence you would like to present?"

"That is all the evidence we have," Deacon Sable said.

Bishop Needly reviewed the petition and the evidence presented. The room was eerily silent. As Bigmama T would say, 'You could have heard a rat piss on cotton.'

After two minutes of silence Bishop Needly began to speak.

"It is my determination that you have not provided sufficient evidence for a formal review hearing and the request is denied," Bishop Needly said. "Are all of you in agreement?" Everyone in the room responded, "Yes."

"There is something I would like to say," I said, as I looked within myself and was shocked that I was even speaking. I stood up from my seat and looked the deacons in the eyes.

"I want you to know that Lance and I love each other very much. I for one do not believe any of these rumors of sexual misconduct involving a man or a woman. He has proven to our family and me that he is a good, respectable Christian man who moves by the Holy Spirit. I know some of you may not have liked all of the changes that he has made this year at New Light, but he needs your support not your venom. If we follow the vision of the Man of God, we will all be blessed. But if we fight him, we will not receive those abundant blessings. Women have tried to lead this church from their houses and you have allowed them to do this at New Light for years. God has ordained male leadership within His church. The church is one of the few institutions where the man is still the hero. But where is he? Where is his leadership? Where is his counsel and wisdom to balance the conversation of church women? I want you to know that we love you and we respect your position within the church. But, I must tell you my heart. These allegations hurt. We live in a world where assumptions and rumors are ruled as fact. Proverbs 22:1 says, 'A good name is more desirable than great riches; to be esteemed is better than silver or gold.' Our family will constantly have to defend ourselves against these allegations and rumors, long after it has been ruled a lie. True Christianity lies in what you do in life when no one else is watching you. My husband, Lance McClain Stevens, is a man of integrity. We need to stand together in solidarity and stomp these attacks from the enemy, Satan seeks to destroy us all. You are the spiritual leaders and protectors of this church and in the future I pray that you all learn to do that together. And learn to pray about conflict before you assume them to be fact to fit your own personal agendas and biases."

I grabbed my purse and walked out into the hallway as my heart pounded within my chest. I thought my chest would explode. I leaned against the wall and exhaled. I heard Bishop Needly lead them in prayer and the men walked out. As the deacons walked past me, they all gave me a hug. I hugged them back. When Deacon Jenkins walked up to me, I fell into his arms in tears.

"I know this was hard, Jackie. But you did great," Jenkins said, as he continued to hold me.

Lance came out of the room and we all stood together. Bishop Needly shook my hand and told Lance that he would have his secretary type the minutes of the meeting and his decision and he would send a copy and file it with the church national headquarters.

In that one meeting, I learned the real pressures of Lance's job. I now understood that our lives were definitely a call from God. And whether I wanted to be included in it or not, I was a part of his ministry. How many corporate wives are called in to sit in on their husband's employee discipline hearing? Not too many, I tell you that. I drove home to find Amanda, my mama, Bigmama T and all three of my children playing a game of Scrabble at the table. I walked in and they all looked at me and invited me to join in the game, and so I did.

Chapter 23

Jesus Will Work It Out

We walked into the processional together as a family that next Sunday morning. I was dressed in a light green apricot dress with matching hat, matching three-inch high-heeled shoes, and an apricot purse. My mother completed my look by surprising me with an apricot Japanese hand fan that she purchased from Neiman Marcus at the Galleria in Houston. The girls were dressed in apricot lace dresses and Junior had a light green Sean Jean suit with matching Stacy Adams shoes. My husband wore a black suit with matching apricot accessories, silk white shirt, apricot tie and handkerchief, and silver apricot cuff links. I walked down the aisle with my husband with my chin strong and our children by our side. Today, was a day to celebrate that Jesus had protected our family and kept us together during our first year at New Light. I looked up at my husband, Pastor Lance McClain Stevens, and had a new respect for him on this day. He looked at me and smiled. The church programs read, "Pastoral Family Appreciation Day!" across the top. There was a biography about Lance and his vision for New Light. There was a list of all of his accomplishments as a preacher and pastor. There were pictures of our family, a small biography about me and a caption of all of our names. Funny, how some things can change over night.

On Saturday, while we were having a barbeque with all of our family members at the community center, we received word that Sister Finley had a massive stroke and had to be rushed to the hospital, late Friday night. Lance and I immediately left the barbeque and rushed to her side. When Lance arrived, Kayla and a flushed Deacon Finley were at Sister Finley's side. Her friend, Betty Jean Pepperdine, sat motionless in a seat by the hospital room door.

"I don't know what happened, Pastor. She was talking on the phone to Deacon Sable late Friday night and she just started complaining about her side hurting her and then she just slumped over," Deacon Finley said.

"Why didn't you call me on Friday?" Lance asked Deacon Finley.

"I just felt so guilty about not showing up to that meeting because I knew what Sarah was up to, but I didn't do a thing about it. I was ashamed, Pastor. I found out last night, that she is the one who authorized all that furniture to be brought to your office. How she managed to get a key to your office and withdraw church funds, I really don't know," Deacon Finley explained, looking like a lost puppy. "I'm sorry that you and your family had to go through all of that."

"Man, we forgive you. We need to see to Sister Finley's needs right now. She needs all of us," Lance said. We looked at Sister Finley and noticed that she was not able to talk. Her body was slouched on one side and she seemed to age by 20 years overnight. We prayed for her that God would heal her and restore the activities of her limbs. Deacon Finley, Kayla, and Betty Jean all cried during the prayer.

As we were exiting, a woman with a new born baby girl and a little boy probably around the age off seven entered the hospital room.

"Monique!" Kayla explained. "What are you doing here?"

"I had to come and see about her. My mama called me and told me that Cousin Sarah had a stroke. I had to come and see about her. I know she told me never to set foot again in Southlake but, I don't care what these people in Southlake think about my children and me. I brought Stewart's new born baby girl for you to see, Cousin Sarah," Monique said as she rushed to Sister Finley's side.

Lance and I quickly turned around as we heard the conversation unfold. *Was this the notorious other woman of New Light's former Pastor Adam Stewart? Was this the legendary Monique Howard? The convention whore known from Houston to El Paso, TX according to the gossip at Heavenly Hands? This woman was related to Sister Finley?* I thought to myself.

Lance looked at me and we both discovered that Sister Finley was more notorious than we originally thought.

Thank you Jesus! That you protected us from the wiles of the enemy! Satan can use anyone to try to destroy Christian believers who truly love the Lord!

Just then, we heard a strange horrid moan rise up from the hospital bed from the lips of Sarah Finley. She rolled her head from side to side. Kayla rushed to her side, she knew that her Aunt Sarah was probably having a fit that her torrid distant cousin, Monique was back in Southlake with her two illegitimate children conceived by the former pastor of New Light, Pastor Adam Stewart who had now retired into seclusion in West Texas and was presently living with his new bride and family.

Lance and I looked at each other and smiled. He reached out to grab my hand as we headed out of Sister Finley's hospital room.

Before leaving the hospital, I had a wonderful idea.

"Lance, have you ever thought about asking Kayla to be the church's administrative assistant?" I asked him, as we drove back to the barbeque.

"You know that is an excellent idea. I'll discuss it with Deacon Jenkins."

So here we are today; walking together as a family in the light of God's love down the middle aisle of New Light. We are a witness that God will take care of His church, His preacher man and his family. I learned through our trials and tribulations that we have been sealed with God's divine protection and favor. God will reward us if we remain faithful to him. Great is the Lord's faithfulness! I have learned over the years that my tongue and anger can only go to so many places; however, my earnest prayers can go to places that I cannot. Our prayers can reach deep into the spiritual realm where the enemy tries to destroy us and entrap us. I am grateful that I have discovered how to watch over my family, embrace my position post in this Christian army, and spiritually grow; it is through the power of much prayer and the reading and application of God's Word in my life.

Dear First Lady,
Today was a beautiful day! The appreciation service was great! Not because we looked good in our clothes but because four souls were saved and restored today! Hallelujah! Brother Graves arranged for Luke Mercer Jr. & Chosen to serve as our special surprise musical

guests and they took the worship to another level! It was an awe-some experience! I am going to have to go and purchase their new CD! And to top it off, gospel artist, Chester D.T. Baldwin strolled in during the service and blessed us with his song, "Another Chance." God knows what we really need! I am so grateful that He is a God of another chance! I don't know how our Minister of Music, Brother Graves, was able to get Luke Mercer Jr. and Chester D.T. Baldwin on the same platform on a Sunday morning, but First Lady as in the words of Bigmama T, "We had some chu'ch, today!" There was not a dry eye in the worship service.

A powerful young preacher from LaMarque, Texas by the name of Pastor C.L. Yancy, Sr. served as the guest evangelist. He preached a powerful sermon called, "A Preacher's Job is Never Done" and the entire church was on its feet! That young preacher can PREACH! The Word of God is powerful and life changing. Vivian Daniels tore the church up with her rendition of Vickie Winans "We Shall Behold Him" during the invitational period. She can give Vickie Winans a run for her money! Ms. Vivian's voice is anointed! She was one of the members who joined our church today! Hallelujah! Jesus will Work it Out!

The kids and I surprised Lance with a painted self portrait of him in his preaching robe by the artist Henry Lee Battle. Lance absolutely loved it and it brought him to tears of joy. It was our children's idea to give their daddy a painted portrait of what he enjoys doing the most, preaching the Word of God!

Sister Finley is still in the hospital and she is still unable to speak. Betty Jean Pepperdine is totally devastated that her life long friend is ill. Kayla has an interview for church secretary with the New Light deacons on Wednesday. Marilyn Steele finally resurfaced and we heard through the grapevine that she has joined another church in Dallas. We still could not figure out who authorized all of our utilities to be cut off during the early part of the week.

Our barbeque on yesterday was awesome. We had over 40 family members ride in or fly in to celebrate with us. All of the New Light deacons and brotherhood provided the food and games. There was not any hint of tension in the air. There was a sweet, sweet spirit of communion in the air at the barbeque that day. Bigmama T, my mama, and Sister Peterson were inseparable during the entire appreciation weekend. By the time, Bigmama T and my mama loaded up to return to Richmond they were humming the tune to Sister Peterson's code word song.

I don't know what Jesus is to you.
But I hope He is to you what He is to me. He's my all, my all and all.
He's my chief cornerstone. I don't know what Jesus is to you,
But I hope he is to you-what He is to me.
They all had a blast together!

I have discovered that my identity is completely found in Christ. Because I have committed my life to Him, there will be constant trials and tribulations in my life, whether I am Mrs. Lance McClain Stevens or not. I have learned to rejoice in this Christian journey and praise God for His blessings that fall like a fresh new rain. I thank God for the seasons of my life as a Christian believer that have come to make me strong. My life as a Christian in the position post of a clergy wife is a life of emerging seasons of growth and maturity. It is in fact a process. I am the student and God is my teacher and every now and then He allows me to instruct the class in the lessons that I have learned from Him; for I am blessed to be a blessing. The evidence of my growth in Christ is found in Proverbs 31:28 concerning a virtuous woman:

Her children arise and call her blessed;
her husband also, and he praises her.

When my children call me blessed and when I can find praise and honor in my husband's eyes that is the proof of my virtue as a mother and wife. I thank God that He is true to His word and He will take care and provide for His own. For the scripture says: "Cast your cares on Him, for he cares for you" First Peter 5:7; and First Lady, I know the Lord definitely cares for me.
Love,
Jacqueline Renee Stevens
And this is my confession.

Jacqueline Steven's Prayer Map

And I will do whatever you ask in my name, so that the Son may bring glory to the Father. You may ask me for anything in my name, and I will do it.

St. John 14:13-14

Prayer: *Please allow Lance to finish seminary*

Answer: *Lance graduated from seminary! We're going to the graduation tonight.*

Prayer: *The parsonage is not suitable for a family. It even leaks when it rains. I pray for us to have a really nice parsonage in the near future*

Prayer: *I pray that one day we will OWN our own home.*

Answer: *It took some time and I have to admit I was getting anxious, but Lance was just appointed Pastor to New Light and God I thank you. The parsonage is absolutely GORGEOUS! Especially with the new paint and the modifications you blessed us to make. I love the prayer nook!*

Prayer: *I met Sister Finley today and I pray the she grows in Christ. I discerned from our conversation that she has some real issues with wanting to run the church's business.*

Ongoing Prayer: *Lord, I pray that you would continue to conform me into your image and mature me so that I can walk worthy of this position you've called me to as a Pastor's Wife, but most importantly as a Christian. I so want to please you in everything I do and say. I have to admit it does get difficult, but I pray that the words of my mouth and the meditation of my heart are acceptable in your sight O' Lord my strength and my Redeemer.*

Prayer: *There is something not quite right about the new lady, Marilyn Steele that joined our church. Please reveal to me if her motives are pure.*

Jacqueline Steven's Prayer Map Cont'd

And I will do whatever you ask in my name, so that the Son may bring glory to the Father. You may ask me for anything in my name, and I will do it. *St. John 14:13-14*

Prayer: *I went to get my hair done today and Vivian was at it again. Just picking me for gossip. I didn't say a word. She did manage to get poor Sister Wiley to tell all her church's business. I pray that you would grow her up as a Pastor's wife quick. She's so young and naïve. Also she seems hurt and troubled about something. Minister to her on a personal level as only you can Father. Also, I pray that Vivian will come back to church.*

Answer & Prayer: *Well, Lord, Sister Marilyn Steele is always in Lance's face and she is moving up rather quickly in the church for someone that is "newly" saved. I thank you that you are revealing to me her true motives. I discern that she and that Sister Finley might be keeping up some mess with our upcoming appreciation program. The kids and I are being completely excluded from the services. They are even acting up about being left out. Especially Junior. He's really mad at his Dad and the church. One more thing, Lord, the Deacon's want to have a meeting with Lance - some sort of allegations. He wants me to go. I pray you go before us and speak through us. I know that no weapon formed against us shall prosper. I thank you in advance for a positive outcome.*

Answers: *Wow, God! Talk about exceedingly above what I could ask or think. The appreciation program was wonderful! We had many souls to join the church including Vivian! I am so happy because you have kept us through such a trying year and we came out with VICTORY! You have brought my family closer to each other and most importantly closer to you. I pray that I can be an example to other First Lady's that you are faithful. We just have to trust you completely!*

Answers: *God, I thank you for moving Marilyn Steele completely out of New Light. She and Sister Finley allowed the enemy to use them with all the appreciation program mess and the allegations against Lance. That meeting with the Deacon's was so unsettling but you brought us through it. It's a shame that Sister Finley ended up having a stroke because of her part in all this. But you did say not to touch your anointed ones. I pray that she will have a complete and speedy recovery and come back to the church with a renewed spirit. This isn't the way I wanted her to grow in you, but Lord you always know what's best. Also, thank you for allowing Sister Wiley to grow in you and I am glad she is no longer angry with me and she's not letting Vivian pick her anymore. I think we just might end up being good friends.*

The First Lady: Confessions of a Preacher's Wife

Discussion Questions

1. What influence do you think Sister Finley's growing up with an alcoholic father may have had on her behavior as an adult?

2. Do you agree that Pastor's wives live in a fish bowl? What if anything can be done so they don't feel so isolated and alone?

3. How important is balance in the life of the believer? What impact might a lack of balance have on a believer's marriage and or family?

4. Deacon Jenkins was called "a friend of the preacher man." How important is it to be supportive of the Pastoral family? What are some ways you can show your support?

5. Do you feel that Sister Finley and Sister Pepperdine's views of the younger women in the church reflect the view of older women in the church toward younger, less churched women? If so, why? How can the gap be bridged between the older and younger women in the body of Christ?

6. Deacon Jenkins indicated that New Light is 75% women. In an age when more and more men or joining churches, why

do you think New Light is still comprised of predominantly female members?

7.   Did Sister Pepperdine fail as a friend to Sister Finley?

8.   As is the case with New Light, more and more "unchurched" people are attending worship services. How should the church handle this new "unchurched" generation entering its walls for the first time? If you were "unchurched" when you joined your church, what did you ministry to do attract and retain you as a new believer/member?

9.   Jackie had her journal as a means of release and a coping mechanism for her daily problems. How important is it to have outlets/coping mechanisms? What outlets do you currently have in place? If none, what can you quickly put in place to assist you in dealing with life's challenges?

10.   Why do you think Lance Sr. was uncomfortable with Junior's display of emotion at the game? How important is it for Father's to express their feelings and love for their children, especially their sons?

11.   Why do you think Lance allowed Marilyn Steele to move up so easily in the church when he knew her history?

12.   Jackie is very open and honest in regards to all of her feelings when praying to God. What can we learn from her transparency in prayer?

13.   Jackie speaks of nurturing a personal relationship with Jesus Christ. How important is it to go beyond church mem-

bership and ritual to truly become intimate with Christ? What are some ways you can deepen your personal relationship with Christ? How can you influence those around you to do the same?

14.   We all know that Satan is after the men of God, much like Pastor Stewart, the former pastor of New Light. What are some ways we can cover our pastor's and the men of God so they don't fall prey to the enemy?

15.   Pastor Stevens established a 501c3 organization and the Victorious Worker's Temp Agency. The agency had a tremendous impact on the community. What are some way's the church can go beyond its walls and make a difference in the community? What gifts and talents do you possess that could be used to assist your church in this area?

16.   Jackie and Lance have truly learned how to take the adversity in their lives and grow from it into more mature Christians. What circumstances has God allowed in your life to mature and prune you? What did you learn from those events and how did they shape you into the Christian you are today? What present circumstance in your life is less than favorable? What Godly characteristic might God be perfecting in your life?

17.   Why do you think Lance was so secretive when it came to divulging information to Jackie? For example, his past with Marilyn Steele, and the anonymous letter he received?

18.   What do you think of Jackie's comments during Lance's informal review with the Board of Deacons?

19. The bible says in I Chronicles 16:22 "Do not touch my anointed ones; do my prophets no harm." Sister Finley violated this biblical warning over and over again; as a consequence she ended up gravely ill. How important is it to watch how we handle the people of God. Have you fallen short in this area? If so, how can you rectify the situation?

20. The triumphant story of the First Lady is a testament to the power of prayer. Please share with the group instances where God moved in your life or the life of a loved one as a result of prayer.

Mikasenoja

For Book Signings and appearances contact:

Mikasenoja

Email: mikasenoja@aol.com

New Hope Bible Baptist Church

3801 McKinney Extension, LaMarque, TX 77568

409-939-9908/409-935-4040

Check out Mikasenoja's new website at

www.mikasenoja.com

Stay tuned for
Mikasenoja's
"The First Lady:
Confessions of a Preacher's Wife"
Volume 2

About the Author

Kimberley Yancy, aka Mikasenoja, Christian fiction's groundbreaking new author, originally hails from Austin, TX and was reared in Galveston County, Texas. Mikasenoja's literary career spans over 15 years, writing such plays as "Holy Ghost Takeover," "Running Back to You," "He's Coming Back Again!" and inspiring columns for Christian magazines across the country. Her debut novel, "The First Lady: Confessions of a Preacher's Wife" is sure to have good church folks talking and reevaluating how they are seen in each other's eyes. Known for her creative story telling, controversial tell-it-like-it-is drama and innovative prose style, Mikasenoja's goal is to empower, equip and encourage the Kingdom of God to live and stand boldly for Christ in an ever-changing society. She hopes to invoke serious discussion and biblical solutions concerning the challenges of the modern day church.

Mikasenoja possesses a compassionate heart of ministry for clergy wives and women church leaders. Mikasenoja holds a B.A. in Government and African-American Studies from the University of Texas at Austin. She currently lives in Texas City, Texas with her husband, Pastor C.L. Yancy, Sr. of eleven years and their four children, Joshua, William, Jennifer and C.J. Currently, Mikasenoja is an employed certified fourth through eighth grade Texas History teacher. Her husband serves as Senior Pastor of the New Hope Bible Baptist Church in LaMarque, TX. Mikasenoja is a proud member of Delta Sigma Theta Sorority, Inc. and strives to exemplify Christ in everything she does in her commitment to God and in serving her community. Her scripture of purpose is, Luke 1:37 "For with God nothing shall be impossible."

Printed in the United States
39219LVS00003B/137